Drawn by the Sea

Drawn by the Sea

Jeanne Davies

Bridge House

British Library Cataloguing in Publication Data
A Record of this Publication is available from the British
Library

ISBN 978-1-907335-82-2

This edition published 2020 by Bridge House Publishing
Manchester, England

For Lindsay, Katie, Sophie, Felicity and James

Contents

Introduction

Most of these stories are written whilst walking for miles in the countryside with my Labrador companion at my side. The beauty of creation and all forms of nature always stirs something in our psyche, whether we acknowledge it or not. To be surrounded by fields, trees and sky in a magnificent green space or wandering along the seashore with the serenity and chaos of the ocean, can inspire and give us peace.

Jeanne Davies

Over the years we have published several of Jeanne's short stories. Indeed, at the end of this volume you will find featured some of the books that contain her work.

Some of the stories published in this volume have also appeared in our anthologies and others are brand new. This is exactly what we like in a single author collection. It's always good, too, to work with an author we know we can trust.

You will find here a mixture of themes and genres. There are brushes with the supernatural, an exploration of human emotions, history, love and loss, and also a firm sense of time and place.

You can really appreciate the inspiration Jeanne refers to above as you read these stories.

Enjoy!

Gill James, editor

Lady of the Water

On that day, the torrents arrived without warning, causing ditches to rise and many of the tiny country roads to become impassable. Rain flung itself like knives at the cloudy windows, hammering down on the old police station as though it was building a new roof. The wind whipped and howled, rattling the old metal window frames and punishing the ancient brass door knocker until it finally crashed onto the doorstep; it's ringing reverberating beneath the stone floor. The winter darkness closed in at four which made storms like these seem endless.

I'd expected rain in that part of the world but had no idea how dramatically and relentlessly it could fall. My journey to these remote parts had been a long and arduous one, including a new career move; but I was determined to leave the past behind me and make a new start. I was really looking forward to retreating to my little rented cottage at the end of my shift. As isolated and lonely as it was, I knew I could sit comfortably with my Kindle before the reassuring wood burner.

At precisely five o'clock, the old station door suddenly flew open, allowing in a deluge of water, born on the wind, which saturated the lobby. A woman appeared from the darkness in a shiny black oil-skin raincoat, a matching southwester hat and red wellington boots. She marched over to the reception desk and stood directly in front of me, her drumming finger nails on the wood sounding like raindrops. Just behind her appeared a scruffy old Airedale terrier who, after a vigorous shuddering, succeeded in shaking a shower of rain droplets from its coarse curly coat, before sitting quietly by the door.

"I'm having trouble with my front door key," she said. "It doesn't work in the lock."

I opened the case book in front of me and started to write the date, asking politely for her address and other details.

"Look, isn't there a male on duty here as I'm not sure a female is quite up to this task?" she said impatiently. "I'm obviously locked out of my home and my husband isn't due back tonight. Tula and I have been walking for hours and both of us need a hot bath… can't someone just come and open the door for me?"

She glared at me before ripping off her hat to allow her long amber hair to cascade across her wet coat and shiver down her back. Her features were refined, with porcelain skin and the darkest of sea green eyes. She could have just stepped out of a John Waterhouse painting.

"Of course," I answered nervously, as any green-horn would. "I just need to take a few details first, madam."

She groaned and gazed impatiently up at the ceiling, crossing her arms in an exaggerated sulk. I thought it strange that there were still strands of liquid trickling down her forehead like worms and that water was seeping from inside her raincoat onto the floor. Clearly not wearing fully protective rainwear I observed self-righteously.

I quickly jotted down as much information as I could extract from her… Delores O'Brien… without angering her any further. I then retrieved our lock equipment whilst quickly heaving on my waterproof boots. I shouted out for Mavis, the telephonist, to man the desk until my return. As usual Mavis was filing her nails with the phone glued to her ear, whilst having a conversation with her husband about what he'd like for tea.

The dog jumped quickly onto the rear seat of the car whilst Delores slid into the passenger seat. Her perfume was unusual; a combination of sweet musk and countryside heather.

11

I was still a novice to the country roads and, despite the rain having suddenly ceased, found it difficult to navigate through flooded tree laden lanes in the dark, especially as the car windows were misted with dog breath. I increased the heater blowing system to high, but Delores sarcastically suggested I'd do better to put my blue light on to guide the way.

"You're new here, aren't you?" Delores asked, without looking at me.

I nodded and told her I'd recently moved from the city to start this new job; in truth, I needed to restart my life.

"A man, I suspect," she detected sourly. "Why else would a pretty young thing like you come to this god forsaken place!"

Ahead we could see Pump Cottage, which was built in flint and had tiny lattice windows peeping shyly over a neat privet hedge.

"Well, there are some lights on!" I said optimistically.

As the car pulled up to the gate, Delores' head suddenly jerked toward me as she grabbed my arm, gripping it tightly. Her deep green eyes focused intently on mine.

"Run, Jenny," she whispered, her face erupting into a deep frown. "Get away from this village as quickly as you can… it's a frightful place and you'll be as good as dead if you stay here."

I felt like a rabbit startled by headlights. Embarrassed, I stared at the floor where a pool of water was welling up in the footwell around Delores' red wellington boots. She released her grip and continued looking straight ahead again. After a confused silence, I grabbed my lock equipment and headed for the front door, prompting the security lantern to flick on.

As any good bobby would, I rang the doorbell first before fiddling with the lock. My heart skipped into my mouth when the door suddenly flung open and a small blonde woman with rosy apple cheeks appeared. She looked at me puzzled; then looked beyond me towards the car.

"Oh, thank you officer... you've bought Tula home!" she said cheerfully.

The little dog, now almost dry from the aggressive car heating system, trotted arthritically past the woman and into the welcoming warmth of the cosy cottage.

"She's been gone for days this time, poor lamb. I've no idea where she goes, but at least she returns to her home eventually."

"But there's this woman..." I began, gesturing back to the car; but Delores had disappeared from the passenger seat.

"I must give her a warm bath," the woman went on. "Thank you so much again, PC Davies," she added sweetly, scrutinising my badge under the porch light. She gently but firmly closed the door, leaving me standing bewildered on the door step.

The car was still fragranced with Delores' perfume but there was no sign of her, just a pool of water in the footwell where she'd previously sat. I searched the front garden and a nearby copse with my flashlight, calling her name into the wind; but there came no response.

By the time I got back to the station it was well after six and Amanda from the night shift had taken Mavis' place at the desk. She'd been reading my notes.

"So, it was Delores, was it then?" she said with a grin.

Before I could answer she suggested I sit down and take a few deep breaths.

"You look very pale, Jenny," she said.

For no apparent reason my body began to shiver and shake, and my teeth started to chatter loudly.

"I'll put the kettle on my dear," she said, pushing me down into the seat and patting her hand on my shoulder.

As the kettle began to purr, Amanda began to relate a story which still confuses me to this day.

"Delores was a city girl like you Jenny," Amanda began. "Her husband 'dumped' her in a country cottage when she became pregnant. He had no time for her really. She was so lonely, poor girl... missed all the hustle and bustle of the city you see and sadly none of her so-called friends ever bothered to visit her. She wasn't interested in making any new friends here of course; we were beneath her, you understand."

She proceeded to make a jug of coffee and landed two mugs on the table.

"The one thing she did like about this place though, were the long country walks. Yes, her and her little dog, Tula, were often seen trekking in remote places – she was an artist you see; funny lot they are!"

I clutched the steaming brew, feeling the warmth bite at my cold palms.

"Apparently, she'd sometimes walk all day long... loneliness can do that to a person, you know. She didn't seem at all excited about having a baby either."

"What happened to the baby?" I asked, burning my tongue on the scorching liquid.

"It died with her I'm afraid."

It took a long time for those words to sink in. I suddenly felt light-headed as the events of the evening began to spin around in my head.

"Apparently she was walking around one of the deep quarries," went on Amanda, sipping her coffee. "When a violent squall came over and they think she was swept in. But talk has it," her voice lowered to a whisper, "that she'd tried to take her own life many times before, poor dear."

14

A vision popped into my head of the sad, pregnant Delores sinking gently into a deep pool, her auburn hair floating briefly like a lily on a pond.

"Tula spends most of her days in the churchyard lying on her grave. Obviously, Frances has been very kind to the little dog and adopted her when she bought Pump Cottage; but Tula still pines for her Delores."

We finished our coffee in silence. Although I'd stopped shaking, I felt freezing cold deep into my bones and totally bewildered.

"So, what you're basically saying then, is that I've just met a ghost?" I said as everything began to sink in. "How many others have seen Delores?"

"A few people say they have seen the woman with beautiful red hair over the years, but no one has ever spoken with her. It seems that not everybody can see her. They usually only notice the dog; you're obviously a sensitive soul... or psychic maybe? Every October fourteenth on the anniversary of Delores' death, little Tula turns up at the station door, just like she's done for the past five years and whoever is on duty returns her to Pump Cottage at the end of their shift. I've never seen Delores myself, but there are many stories about her around here."

"But one more question Mandy... how did Delores know my name?"

She paused for a moment, seeming puzzled.

"Easy dear... she saw your name badge!"

But when I glanced down, my badge just said PC J Davies... no mention of Jenny.

I did leave the village eighteen months later. I only stayed on in the hope that I'd meet poor Delores again, but it never happened. When out and about doing my duties, I occasionally visited her abandoned grave and, as usual, little Tula lay curled up there, barely visible amongst the long unkempt grass.

However, on the next October fourteenth, I'd ensured I was on duty again. At about five o'clock there was a strange scratching noise at the door. I opened it anxiously, allowing a sudden gush of wind into the station. It was thick with the fragrance of Delores' perfume but there was no sign of her. Then in from the blackness trotted Tula and the fragrance gradually faded. At the end of my shift, somewhat disappointed, I dutifully returned Tula into Frances' safe hands at Pump Cottage.

I moved back to the city and became part of the Metropolitan police force. I didn't miss the bleakness of the landscape, nor the recurrent gunmetal skies. I met my soul mate, Andrew, and we married within a year. It was a busy life and I'd almost forgotten about my ghostly experience, when a flyer came into the station with the normal influx of mail. I snatched it off my assistant's desk and a tingle of excitement whizzed down my spine... it was a photograph of the lovely Delores. I took it home that evening to show Andy, who I felt had never quite believed my eerie little story. There was an exhibition of her paintings at a gallery nearby and I dragged my dubious spouse along to see it that weekend.

I was mesmerised by Delores' rich dark oil paintings. You could track the course of her life from her busy London high society life with elegant parties, where her paintings depicted women holding cocktails and cigarette holders, to her confinement in the bleak countryside of North Wales.

There was one particular painting in her collection, a bright water colour that immediately brought tears to my eyes. It was of Pump Cottage, where her key wouldn't work in the door that day. The front garden was full of summer blooms and an abundantly flowering deep pink rose

16

climbed in an arch over the doorway. In the garden was an old Silver Cross style pram and beside the handles sat Tula, upright and protective on a little wooden stool.

My hands instinctively went to my belly and I cradled my small bump as I realised that, if it hadn't been for dear Delores' haunting visit, I'd still be stuck in that god forsaken place.

The Day the Pony Went

Liz stirred to the tinkering of china cups coming from downstairs and guessed that Roger was making early morning tea. She rubbed the sleep from her eyes, listening to the faint sounds of morning drifting in from the farmyard. As she rolled over in the spring sunlight piercing through the yellow curtains, it dawned on her that today was the day Scrumpy was going. With a tear trickling down her cheek and a smile playing on her lips, she reminisced about the fun they'd had with the little pony over the past twenty years. She then consoled herself; the fact was that Scrumpy had always been a very naughty horse... and still was.

"What time are they arriving?" Roger asked as he juggled with a tray at the half open bedroom door.

"Not 'til four."

"Does Sophie know it's today?"

"I think she's hoping it won't happen; yesterday she tried to persuade me to keep her until the grandchildren arrive."

"Well, that won't happen for a while; Martin's got his career to think about," said Roger, landing the tray clumsily on the dresser.

Liz glared at him, her eyes chastising him for the spilt liquid in the saucers.

"We can't go on like this, Roger," she tutted, briskly mopping up the mess with a handful of tissues. "Scrumpy's been having a terrible influence on Fred lately; no, she will have to go today and that's final."

After breakfast Liz wrapped herself up warm before venturing out to feed the goats and chickens; she then went on to clean out the stables. Fred seemed subdued today and didn't protest whilst she brushed him down. She stood back admiring his deep mahogany coat gleaming in the sunshine.

"You really *are* a handsome fellow!" she affirmed with a grin.

Fred's dark seal-like eyes gazed solemnly ahead at the stable door. Liz threw down the brush and decided to cheer him up with some cantering around the field. His hooves crunched rhythmically on the icy smattering of snow. She always found it a pleasure to ride this big powerful bay as he'd once been a top eventer and was all of 16.3 hands tall. It was a shame to stable him again, but today she needed to focus her attention on the pony.

Scrumpy, a New Forest bay, was much shorter and stouter than Fred, especially in her winter coat. Her flaxen mane and tail stood out against her chestnut hide like an Irish coffee. She'd dumped anyone she didn't approve of, apart from Sophie. She detested all other children but scorned adults even more, once deserting Liz on the side of a road before trotting back home without her.

"I know you're a wicked horse, yet I shall be sorry to see you go," whispered Liz into the pony's twitching ear.

The rough and stocky pony whinnied and peeled her lips back, revealing a row of yellow tombstone teeth. Ignoring the devilish look in Scrumpy's eye, Liz allowed her to nuzzle her jacket for the apple in her pocket. She reflected on all the fun they'd had over the years, despite her behaviour at children's' parties when she flatly refused to allow any of Sophie's friends to mount her. Scrumpy also had a deep hatred for their grounds-man, Reg, often taking it upon herself to destroy items of his equipment and clothing. She'd once eaten right through the padding of his car seat when he inadvertently left the door open.

Roger was busy cleaning up Scrumpy's horse box for the new owners. He nostalgically polished the plaque which Sophie had made years ago with Scrumpy's name on it.

Fred was watching Roger intently with his head leaning over his stable door.

If Scrumpy hadn't been so risky, Liz would have taken her for a final canter, but she decided to play it safe and lead-walk her to the nearby water meadows at Churchy Meads, before returning her for a good grooming. She carefully put on the pony's brightly coloured head collar and lead-rope and wistfully took one last photograph for her daughter. She whistled for Emma, the Collie, and Humphrey their young Dalmatian, to join them.

They crunched noisily over puddles turned into bewitched glass overnight, scattering snow perched precariously on naked trees which threatened to drop down in any whisper of wind. Emma, being a very sensitive animal, walked close to Liz's heal but Humphrey streaked ahead through mushy snow, causing a veritable blizzard with his long whipping tail.

The sun sliced through a crack in the powdery cloud like a torch from heaven and the light changed to a haunting silver hue, which bounced off a silver Mercedes apparently left there by walkers. Liz found it curious that there was a pile of clothes folded neatly on the bonnet; perhaps someone was bravely taking an icy dip nearby.

Before she could stop him, Humphrey dashed over to the car and began dragging the clothing to the floor. Emma ran over to rescue them but instead the Dalmatian and Collie picked up an arm each of a man's tweed sports jacket and danced across the meadow in a tug of war. Quickly dropping the pony's leading reign, Liz tore after the dogs, only to find the Saville Row jacket had a gaping hole beneath each armpit. She scolded both dogs and quickly put Humphrey on his lead. As she turned back towards the car she saw to her horror that the pony had foraged through the pile of soggy clothes and found a rather smart broad-rimmed ladies country hat. Scrumpy was lovingly creating a fringe around the brim with her teeth, whilst the tartan bow dangled limply in shredded tatters. Liz tried to grab the hat, which was made by Burberry, but Scrumpy's jaw clamped hard down on her prized possession. She tried to peer through the car windows, but they were all steamed up. Seeing nobody was about, she very carefully rearranged the clothes back on the bonnet of the car, hiding the sports jacket at the bottom of the pile. In order to make a speedy getaway, Liz realised they'd have to take the hat with them.

She sighed with relief as the farm cottage materialised ahead with a bright rainbow arched over its roof. She took this as an optimistic sign that today Scrumpy would indeed be sold and would be leaving them for a good life with a new young family.

Scolding her again, Liz put Scrumpy into the paddock for her last afternoon at Thurlestone Farm… hat grasped intently between the horse's premolars. She headed to the kitchen to put the kettle on, tossing a few crumpets on the Aga, before slumping exhausted into the nearest chair and closing her eyes. Her heart rate had just begun to calm when Roger burst into the kitchen looking ashen.

"You forgot to put the extra chain on Fred's stable door, Liz!" he said, with a forehead full of furrows.

Fred had used his teeth many times to open the door but today Liz had been so preoccupied with the pony leaving, she'd forgotten to chain it. They both rushed outside in time to witness Fred effortlessly clearing the fence, galloping across Scrumpy's paddock and then trotting proudly over to nuzzle her. Scrumpy seemed delighted as they snuggled each other's manes. As soon as Liz and Roger went over, they both began to tear recklessly around the paddock together in some sort of frenzied race.

"Sheee's responsible for this!" Liz bellowed, pointing a

21

finger at Scrumpy. "We must get Fred stabled again quickly, Roger."

There was a feverish chase around the paddock with Liz screeching at the top of her voice at Scrumpy and her husband, narrowly missing a three-way collision. The horses were fast and excited, Fred flipping back his lips in an exaggerated smile. Scrumpy clung on to the Burberry hat as they nodded their heads to each other, repeatedly whinnying with their warm breath snorting clouds from flared nostrils. Their galloping hooves thundered past in a magnificent dance, churning up the paddock into a brown stew. Liz and Roger stood bewildered in the centre of what appeared to be a circus ring. Eventually Fred paused and calmly sauntered over to his breathless owners to accept a carrot.

"I'm surprised at you, Fred," Liz reprimanded as she secured the extra stable door chain.

The smell of burning crumpets radiated from the kitchen.

"You go, I'll see to Scrumpy," Roger instructed.

Liz entered the smoke-filled kitchen, tripping over the cat as it dashed passed her. She slipped and slid as she realised that Felix had knocked a whole churn of butter milk over when making his escape. It took some while for Liz to clean up the mess and calm herself down. Roger came in from grooming Scrumpy and put a hand on her shoulder.

"She's groomed and ready to go, dear."

A car was slowly making progress along the bumpy gravel drive. Liz regarded herself in the mirror before fixing on a fake smile and going out to greet Scrumpy's buyers. The silver Mercedes looked somewhat familiar and she realised to her horror that it was the one parked at the water meadows. A short, well dressed, blonde woman in her mid-forties walked towards Liz, followed by a man of a similar age wearing a dishevelled tweed jacket. Liz felt the colour rise to her cheeks.

"Hello... Mrs. Mills?" asked the woman. "I believe we've come to buy your pony."

Liz was speechless and glued to the spot. The woman glanced over Liz's shoulder and a look of disbelief washed across her face. Roger was leading Scrumpy out to greet the new owners... with the Burberry hat still dangling from her mouth.

"Is this some sort of joke?" the woman asked through thin curled lips, her face turning bright red.

After the couple left, Liz and Roger sat in the pantry with a large glass of wine.

"The day the pony went," said Roger with a smile.

"Although she didn't go, because the buyers stormed off and sped down the driveway as though the car wheels might catch fire!" Liz laughed.

A week later, two girls turned up with their parents. They were twins and about the same age as Sophie had been when they'd first bought Scrumpy. They took an immediate shine to the pony as Sophie had done, stroking her, cuddling her and feeding her sugar cubes they'd brought along with them. Liz watched in amazement as Scrumpy trotted amiably around the compound with both girls on her back. Tears welled in her eyes as memories of her daughter and her beloved pony came flooding back. This stubborn horse had clearly been waiting for these girls, and she was in her element with them; she had chosen them... just like she did with Sophie all those years ago.

"Would you believe it, Liz!" Roger said breathlessly after they'd left. "They were so pleased, they paid the whole amount in cash so they could take her today!"

"Just as well... they've no idea what they're letting themselves in for," Liz whispered.

Waiting for the Light

Longchenpa slowly detached himself from the sphere of light. He'd just witnessed another life lost in the pursuit of truth. He felt spiritually drained, but his scrawny half-naked body remained poised on the square plinth. From high in the green Himalayan Mountains he could see all the struggles of mankind through his box of light.

The sun began to lower in the sky and he anticipated the gift of nourishment. A young monk entered the temple carrying a small tray. His movements felt like a gentle breeze and Longchenpa inhaled the aroma of jasmine flowers. He could sense the sweat on the monk's brow, hear the dust falling from his feet and feel the energy of the outside world. The Samanera bowed and scraped his chin along the floor beneath the Lama as he crawled backwards from the sanctuary.

Longchenpa sighed as he sunk into his renewed isolation. The journey he had chosen many years ago had led him to achieve the ultimate goal of a Buddhist monk, to attain liberation from suffering through his self-discipline. He had lived one hundred years this way, seeking absolute enlightenment through the box of light, just as his teacher had and many others before him, all longing for that illuminating void.

As the cup touched his lips the fragrant smell of jasmine entered each nostril. The delicious liquid slipped down, soothing his throat and energising his fragile transience. Through his tiny single window, he watched the cloak of dusk falling, creating shadows and swirling mists through the coniferous forests beyond. In the distance tall firs lined the ridge of the emerald mountains like attentive choir boys.

Soon strands of silver moonlight aligned themselves upon him and night descended in a dark veil. He inhaled deeply and held on to the breath, allowing every morsel of oxygen to be absorbed by brain and body. He closed his eyes to blind himself from the moon and tried to imagine the hours of daylight that he had, once again, deprived himself of. He visualised the innocent dawn, writing its dazzling message across the sky and gradually dimming all the heavenly bodies. He imagined the feel of warm sunshine on his face.

Longchenpa felt lifted above the restrictions of mortality and was awakened to an affinity with the universe. In his mind's eye he walked barefoot upon cooling moss on a path through long grasses and ferns. He entered a field of ripening corn where tiny fluorescent damsel flies darted in and out of flowing wheat like small fish; he could sense the gentle murmur of their invisible wings.

He transformed himself into a huge bottle-green dragonfly, his elegant sapphire tail extending far behind him as he flew. He looked left and right to admire his luminescent wings, their transparency allowing only his shadow to reveal his presence against the thickly wooded emerald mountains.

At last he was free!

He manoeuvred close beside a young musk deer, frocked in innocence and walking gracefully on stilettoed feet across the fauna. Momentarily her huge lash-adorned globes glanced across at him, bowing her long neck in curiosity. His six feet attached to several pink hooded flowers of Himalayan Balsam, draped in heart shape leaves. He sped on, reluctantly leaving the sweet-smelling sticky nectar behind. A white butterfly flurried along erratically beside him, searching for Temple Magnolia; her paper-thin wings blinked camaraderie at him.

Longchenpa then took the form of a mighty Himalayan

Griffon with a large noble golden beak. His enormous cream feathered wings spread majestically beside him as he soared high above tea plantations neatly cultivated in endless rows along the mountain. Women up to their necks in bushes wore wicker baskets strapped to their hats as they stretched out to pick the delicate new leaves. Some gazed up at him and smiled, their hooded eyes alight with wonder.

He glided over rivers glistening from nearby glaziers, all snaking vibrantly through the lush green pastures. A family of snow leopards knelt cautiously to drink from the effervescent waters with their long, spotted tails lifted perpendicular for balance. The bigger of the ghost cats raised its dramatic head to look up at Longchenpa; he flew on past, not fooled by their endearing features.

Up and up he ascended until he reached the ice-covered mountains, his pale powerful shape barely visible against the snow. He found himself above the mighty Everest, the forehead of the sky. He marvelled at the majestic giant named 'Holy Mother' by his people.

After a while, Longchenpa was aware that he'd escaped the earth's gravity, leaving the problems of mankind far behind. He was shrouded in lights which thickly dotted the velvet blackness. Stars mingled within his feathers as his wings began to glide effortlessly into ethereal silence. A great peace fell upon him.

In the distance he could see an apparition, opaque and almost invisible. He was drawn in closer to it. The light caught in every angle of the face like a mirror with many facets. Its hair consisted of rainbow coloured strands, continually changing shape in tiny wafts of light from the atmosphere. It sat at the edge of a great basin-shaped hole where raging fires intermittently released huge white balls of fire out into the atmosphere.

A voice radiated from the strange being. *"Do you claim to be a spiritual guide?"* it asked.

Longchenpa found he was unable to speak; but the being somehow understood his inner thoughts.

"You must help the world before it is too late; time is short for you, but you choose to distance yourself from these things. Before long the human race will destroy itself with war and conflict."

With these words a strange sadness haunted the spectre and tears glistened in its eyes. Feeling no fear, Longchenpa pleaded for knowledge as to what he should do.

"Perhaps you must be weakened in order to understand the human condition and to appreciate humility," it responded. *"It is your duty to empower the innocent with your wisdom... to give them a voice."*

Without warning Longchenpa was plunged into complete blackness. A stark coldness began creeping through him, slowly invading every inch of his body. Asphyxiated and paralysed; no breath could go in or out of his lungs. He was suspended in a bottomless blackness, a deep empty void. At any moment he thought he might lose consciousness but instead he remained frozen and his thoughts plummeted into a giant pool of great sadness. It was a terrifying place filled with negativity and great emptiness, where nothing, least of all hope, existed. He knew then that he must be dead.

After what seemed like an eternity, Longchenpa's eyes gradually opened. He found himself back in his sanctuary... back in his chosen place of isolation from the world.

"As every flower fades, there is the knowledge that the plant will bloom again," the creature's voice echoed all around him.

He knew then that no matter how temporary life was, there would always be a constant… a creator watching over mankind and the equilibrium of the universe.

"Only love is real," Longchenpa muttered under his breath. Then he fell into a deep sleep; he slept like he had never slept before in his whole life.

When he awoke, things felt very different. He felt a sudden urgency to tell everyone about what he'd encountered. He realised that, although it was important to attain liberation from suffering for oneself, he must work to ensure enlightenment for the sake of others. He realised he must teach them to first establish peace within their minds by training in spiritual paths, so that outer peace would come naturally; otherwise world peace could never be achieved.

Longchenpa knew he did not have all the answers, but tomorrow he, the Lama, would take his place once again as Guru and gather his villagers around him. He would stare into the children's beautiful upturned faces and choose his protégés to pass the wisdom he had learned onto. From now on he decided that he would move amongst the people of the whole world to guide and teach them to love one another, live in peace and to flourish.

Longchenpa would live this way until the end of his days… no longer waiting for the light.

"I never see what has been done; I only see what remains to be done" – Buddha

Family Ties and Little lies

It had been years since I'd heard from Ann, so it came as quite a shock when she phoned out of the blue one day. We used to be such good friends when we were growing up in the same tiny village.

"Darcy, Mum died on Friday," she sobbed into the phone. "David's working in South Africa for three months and I don't think I can cope alone."

"Oh, I'm so sorry Ann. What about your sister, it was her mum too?"

"I haven't heard a thing from Louise; not that I would expect help from her anyway. Please come and stay... I would really value your sagacity."

If I were honest, I felt quite put out that Ann was expecting me to drop everything to help her organise Daphne's funeral. I'd always been there for Ann, even at school when she was often the butt of cruel jokes about her weight. Although she was a pretty child with a blonde mane of hair, Ann had always taken refuge in food, especially sugary foods like doughnuts and cakes when she was feeling depressed. But I realised that her lack of confidence mainly stemmed from having a bully of an older sister.

Of course I did drop everything and made my way down to Sussex and the little village of Tangmere, which was nestled beneath the South Downs. My family had lived next door to her Auntie Alice, and we'd attended the same school there. In her teens, Ann moved to London to work as an accountant where she later married a wealthy banker, before settling back in Sussex. In my teens, my family moved to Shropshire and so I'd only visited Ann for the odd christening, marriage or death. Ann and I had been in touch much more whilst our families were young, and she had visited us with her children during summer vacations to enjoy the Shropshire countryside.

I drove along the winding country lanes of Sussex which were still imprisoned in the grip of winter. Nothing seemed to have changed in the sleepy little parish of Tangmere. There were some new housing estates on the outskirts of the village, but still only one shop, one pub and the little Saxon church where Ann had been married; with me as her maid of honour. She lived at the Old Vicarage; a picturesque family home built in flint with a grey slate roof and wisteria-framed Georgian windows.

"How are you dear?" I asked as I hugged her. Her eyes looked haunted and she'd lost weight.

"I'll be better now that you're here, dear Darcy," she said. "You know it's even harder to lose a second parent… you feel so alone, like an orphan."

"Well, you're not alone," I assured her. "But where are those lovely children of yours?"

"They're all assembling here next week for the funeral. Katie is stateside and Libby's still in Canada."

"And how about my lovely godson?"

"He's in the middle of dissertation work in Plymouth, so I wouldn't expect him to turn up until he really has to," she said glumly.

"Well, that's why *I'm* here, my dear Ann."

"Make yourself at home and I'll put the kettle on," she said.

I wandered into her spacious living room, picking up a photo of us both as school girls. Ann soon appeared rattling two cups and saucers, the fragile sunlight revealing the true extent of her swollen eyes.

"I won't let the dogs in yet as they always knock things over," she said glancing through the French windows at two adorable middle-aged chocolate Labradors. She managed a brief smile.

"They must be company for you."

30

"Yes, they are, Darcy. In fact, ever since Mum died, I've been walking them every couple of hours! It feels like my legs are going to fall off... but it helps."

"You've not spoken to Louise then?"

Ann frowned into her tea cup. "Well, you know how it's always been between us," she said.

"Still poor communications between the two of you?"

"None at all, really. Darcy." She paused. "I do have a confession to make though. I especially hoped that you would be here today as Louise intends to pop in later."

She looked at me with a half-baked smile; but I could tell she was terrified. I'd never got on with Louise. She'd always been a very condescending person who relished being cruel, especially to her sister. Most of our childhood conversations had been short and basically civil, but I'd always tried to protect Ann against Louise's bullying.

"Did she see much of Daphne?"

"I think you know the answer to that!" she replied, putting her cup and saucer on the coaster which protected the highly polished coffee table. "Strangely enough, Mum told me she visited her suddenly out-of-the blue about three months ago and they went out to Victoriana's. Mum didn't say much about the visit, except that the tea shop had really gone downhill, as her fingers were covered in dust when she left. I hope they made their peace with each other then, for Mum's sake more than anything. Anyhow, it's too late now."

The doorbell rang. Ann threw me a nervous look and rose swiftly from her chair, taking her tea cup noisily with her.

"Sis! How's it going dear?" came the familiar but commanding voice from the hallway. "I read yesterday that when the second parent pops their clogs, the kids can finally relish the true taste of freedom..." her voice tapered off as

31

she entered the living room. "Darcy," she said tersely, immediately turning her back to me.

"So sis, I've come to assist with the said funeral arrangements – now… give me a job. After all, we need to give the old bat a good send off, don't we?" She smirked as she sat down and lit a cigarette. "Must keep up appearances after all."

Ann didn't respond but stood there with a panicked look on her face.

"Do you still live in London?" I asked.

Louise ignored me. "One would appreciate a coffee from one's sibling… if that's at all possible?"

Ann rushed to the kitchen.

Louise previously had at least three marriages to my knowledge and countless affairs under her belt. She'd always wanted to be an actress and, as she was childless, lived in a smart penthouse in the centre of the city. She worked as a theatrical agent. I had briefly come into contact with her a year ago whilst working for the prosecution on a fraud case. She'd made it clear that she either didn't recognise me or refused to acknowledge who I was.

So, dear sis… were you brave enough to visit the morgue?"

No; I'd prefer to remember Mum as she was when she was alive and well," Ann said, shrugging her shoulders humbly and carefully placing Louise's coffee on a coaster.

"Well, I just had to go," Louise said, stubbing her cigarette out in a nearby plant pot. "Had to make sure the old bag had definitely demised… finally!"

It was a painful afternoon with little achieved, other than the complete disintegration of Ann in floods of tears after Louise left. I suggested we walked the dogs and so we tramped through muddy fields with naked trees shivering in the north-east wind like witches' brooms. I was taken aback by how fast she could walk, clearly driven by emotion. After many tears, I suggested we go to the pub for supper and leave her cottage pie in the fridge for another day.

"On Wednesday, we have the reading of mum's will – will you come?" she begged, downing the dregs of her wine glass.

"Of course, that's no problem. Malcolm is perfectly fine without me. He has much to do in his workshop at the moment, so he probably won't even notice I've gone!"

Ann managed a grin.

"Do you think it would be alright for me to visit your Auntie Alice whilst I'm down?"

"Oh, she would adore seeing you Darcy– she's always liked you. Do you remember her delicious home-made cookies?"

"Yes... I can also remember Louise took handfuls of them, only leaving a few for us!"

The following day I set out for the Barchester Care Home where Alice had lived for several years now, leaving Ann busy with catering details for the wake.

"Darcy dear!" she squeaked, closing her book and rising nimbly from a high-backed chair to hug me. "How wonderful to see you... it's been ages."

Alice must have been in her mid-eighties but looked amazingly fit and slim. She was a widow from a happy but childless marriage, so perhaps that explained it. Her silver hair was cut into a fashionable bob which framed her impish face.

"You look amazing; and this is such a lovely place," I said.

"Yes, it is; but I am so heartbroken to lose Daphne, my baby sister," she said. "Much too sudden for my liking – only a few weeks ago she visited me and looked like a young filly."

33

"It's awful when it's so unexpected," I reflected. "Ann is really finding it difficult with Henry away, so I've come down to support her through the funeral arrangements."

"Humph... Henry!" she tutted. "You always were a good friend to her, Darcy; sadly, she never got on with her sister. But then, I feel sorry for Louise... such a mixed-up kid. She's my goddaughter and I shall be leaving everything to her in my will."

"But what about Ann?"

"She's done so well for herself, not just financially but having three beautiful children. Louise is alone and has nothing in comparison. I think she always believed Daphne preferred Ann, and it gave her a chip on her shoulder. Perhaps my little nest egg might make her feel loved after all."

"Do you keep in touch with Louise then?"

"Oh, no she never visits or writes, but Daphne would have wanted me to help her; that's why she made me her Godmother."

We reminisced about my childhood over several cups of Earl Grey and then I hugged her before making my way back to Tangmere.

Wednesday came and Louise was noticeably absent from the solicitor's office so it was just Ann and I who heard Daphne's will read. The shock to both of us was enormous... she had left everything to her elder sister Alice.

"This is a most unusual case," remarked the solicitor. "Usually the children and grandchildren would receive all the benefit from a parent's estate. Clearly your Aunt is in her eighties and... well... may not be able to appreciate the funds in quite the same way."

"She did tell me a long time ago that she didn't want to leave anything at all to Louise," said Ann looking bewildered.

"I suppose Auntie's care home does cost a great deal of money, and she knew I didn't want for anything. But my children... her grandchildren?"

"With all due respect to the deceased, to change her will so suddenly and without obtaining advice from us was ridiculous to say the least," the solicitor said. "There would have been other ways of dealing with a situation like this."

"She changed her will recently then?" I asked.

"Yes, the new system allows a person to make changes through the internet, without their legal representative being present. The document requires a signature and also a finger print for security, which as you can see has been fulfilled."

"When did you receive this document?" I asked, passing it along to Ann.

"It arrived here on the ninth of March and was filed with all her previous documents."

"That's just under two months ago," I concluded. Ann looked bewildered.

"Are we allowed to see the previous will?"

"No, I think that under the circumstances it would be most upsetting for her daughter."

Ann was in a sombre mood as I drove us back to the Old Vicarage.

"I didn't want or need anything anyway," she finally said in a croaky voice. "It's just I would have liked her to leave me something sentimental – valueless, but personal."

"What did you mean back there about your mum not wanting to leave anything to Louise?" I asked.

"It's a really long story," she replied.

"Let's walk the dogs and discuss it," I suggested as we pulled into her driveway. "Only not at such a fast pace today please!"

As we walked along together it all became quite clear. It

transpired that Ann's mother, Daphne, had given birth to Louise out of wedlock; but even more surprisingly to me, Ann and Louise did not share the same father. This had been dug up and exposed by Louise just prior to her father (or stepfather) dying. The scandal had upset the old man so much that Daphne was sure it had caused his sudden and fatal heart attack. Daphne's contact with Louise had already been limited but from then on it was completely terminated... until three months ago.

"I just don't understand why mum wouldn't have given me a hint – I thought we were so close." Tears began to well up in Ann's eyes again.

The funeral went off as well as could be expected. Henry disappeared back to his project in South Africa the following day, but Ann said she was fine for me to return home to Malcolm. All the same, I did so with a heavy and sad heart for Ann.

It was a few weeks later that I received another call from Ann.

"Auntie Alice has died," she said in a small voice. "Can you come and stay again? The children have all gone back to their lives and Henry is still away... sorry Darcy."

"Don't worry. I'm sure Malcolm will be fine in his workshop again – he managed OK last time on a freezer full of cottage pie and pizza!"

Alice's funeral was a brief service at the crematorium, unlike Ann's mother's wonderful church service and dignified burial with all the family present. Louise had been aloof at her mother's funeral and had decided not to return to Ann's house for the wake. However, she was larger than life at Alice's wake, which was held at the care home; she managed to be her usual arrogant self.

Alice's last will and testament had been an even bigger shock to Ann; Alice had left all her worldly goods (including

Daphne's legacy) to Louise as her goddaughter. Again, nothing sentimental was left for Ann to hang on to, which wounded her greatly.

Louise kissed her sister theatrically before taking her leave from the solicitors office. "I guess the best sibling won after all, sis," she said spitefully.

"Oh, Louise," I said pulling her to one side whilst Ann visited the bathroom. "I'm very worried about Ann and wondered if you would consider coming back to her house with us for a bit?"

"Oh, I'm sorry," she replied mockingly. "Things not going quite to plan for my dear little sister, I presume?"

"Well, I believe things are not as they might seem with these deaths and the two wills – I have something very interesting to show you," I said persuasively.

"Oh, now I am intrigued," she said, lighting a cigarette. "I guess I can delay my return to London for an hour." She turned away to use her mobile phone.

"Where exactly is the little sis?" Louise said haughtily as I led her through the hallway to Ann's living room.

"She'll be down in a minute," I said. "Do have a seat."

"Do I get offered a cup of coffee this time, or must I beg for it again?" she scoffed.

"I don't think coffee is applicable this time Louise," I answered curtly. "I believe you will soon be drinking coffee in prison."

She let out a gasp. "How dare you!" she said, jumping to her feet.

"No, sit down Louise," I said firmly. "There is something I want you to hear before your sister comes down." She obeyed for once. "I know that you killed your mother!"

"What?"

"I said, I know that you killed your mother," I reiterated calmly.

"What absolute rubbish... I always knew you were a silly cow!"

"You visited your mother three months before her death and you took her to that special tea shop she loved, didn't you?"

"So?"

"You weren't in the habit of visiting your mother very often, were you Louise?" I said skirting around the highly polished coffee table.

"Well, Mother and I never did get on much... she preferred little sis and that was perfectly clear."

"I understand from the tea shop that two cups were broken on the day of your visit. Is that correct?"

"I can't remember. I think it was just the silly old bag's cup actually," she said, grabbing a cigarette between pursed lips.

"No, Louise it was your cup that broke, but the tea room realised afterwards that the other one went missing."

There was a silence as she inhaled heavily on the cigarette.

"So, exactly what's that got to do with anything?"

"I believe you removed your mother's cup and took it back to London with you."

"I can assure you, darling, I have enough cups in my own cupboard to last a lifetime... I'm not a pauper you know!"

"Oh no, I understand that... you're definitely not a pauper Louise; and from now on you should be a seriously rich woman living off the estates of both your aunt and your mother. But you needed that cup as it held your mother's finger prints, didn't it?"

She smirked but didn't respond.

"I believe your mother asked you to visit her because she knew she was terminally ill and had only months to live," I went on.

"What? I didn't know that," interrupted Ann as she appeared like a ghost at the sitting room door.

"I also believe that Daphne told you that you would not be featured in her will and that everything would be left to Ann, apart from the identity of your father... which was to be her parting gift to you."

"Yes, and the bastard bloody well died before I could see him anyway... leaving all his estate to his new children. But what about me, eh? Why should I always be the one who gets left out?" she shouted as she rose to her feet. She stubbed her cigarette aggressively onto Ann's polished coffee table and muttered, "A bloody house should always have ashtrays!"

She stood still for a moment and I could almost hear the cogs running around in her brain.

"Well... you can't prove a thing. You just can't prove one bloody thing!" she said with glee.

"I know we can't," I said calmly, "but maybe it's the lawyer in me that needs to know how you did it and how nobody suspected – you already knew Alice had made you sole heir to her estate, because she'd written to you."

"Oh fine then! Mother was dying anyway... the old bag. She didn't want "little sissy" to know because it might 'upset' her whilst she was having problems in her marriage – yes, she told me that too," she said as she swung around to confront Ann. "So much for the perfect couple... you and Henry; it appears that little sis couldn't hold it together any more than I could!" she mocked.

"I am so sorry," I said turning to Ann, who had flushed with anger as much as shock. I hadn't known about this part of the puzzle.

"It only needed a bigger dose of morphine," she went on blatantly. "I knew they wouldn't bother with an autopsy under the circumstances.

"So you visited your mother again?" I asked.

"Yeh, it was *my* goodbye gift, shall we say. Anyway, I gave her a good send off, the old bag, which was more than she deserved!" she said callously. "Classy tea at her favourite tea shop with as many cakes as she desired, then a long soporific end."

Silence filled the room like a foul-smelling odour.

"Well then; I'm off back to London leaving "little sissy" to get on with her divorce," she added viciously.

"Oh no, I don't think so," I said walking towards the French windows. "Of course, you have met Detective Inspector Randall I believe... he used to be the village bobby when we were all growing up. He has recorded every bit of this conversation, Louise."

Louise let out a sudden gasp, allowing a cascade of white cigarettes to tumble from the packet.

"Therefore," I went on, "we do not need to prove that you took your mother's fingerprints off her cup after leaving the tea shop, using graphite powder – which explains why her fingers were so dusty when she arrived home; and she thought the tea room was dirty! We don't need to prove that you faked a new will on the internet, forging your mother's signature and using the finger print from the tea cup to comply with the extra security."

Louise was speechless, for the first time in her life.

"In addition to this," I added, "your aunt's care home has recently been involved in some medical investigations as they believe that Alice's death was not an accident either. But then you would know all about that already, wouldn't you, Louise?"

She tried to make a run for the door, but DI Randall dashed towards Louise and grabbed her arm. He then uttered those classic words:

"I think you'd better come with me, Miss!"

I Found Her

She was in the meadow dancing; tall and slender with long tresses falling to her waist. She was at one with the breeze, floating, twirling and waving at birds.

I saw her many times; poised and burnished by summer sun, dancing in violent winds, or bare bones arched against the storm.

Much time passed before I saw her again. I then found her gnarled and care worn; her movements stiff and slow.

I found her again; she'd been cut down.

Soon she would be burnt, and her ashes scattered. But once again I hoped she would dance in the wind.

Shadowlands

She spun around as the key jolted abruptly in the lock; her heart gave a sudden flip in her chest. With a pulse building in her ears, Libby rattled the door handle, calling out for Reg to let her out, but he didn't respond. She hovered beside the door, feeling beads of sweat prickle in a starburst across her forehead. Her saliva-coated tongue hung limp and unruly in her mouth. She choked on a scream as sobs caught in her throat.

Panic welled inside her as she desperately scanned the room. Reg kept the windows locked... and she knew they were all double glazed. Gulping like a goldfish for air, she began beating her fists feverishly against the door, her cheeks flushed and soaked with tears.

"Someone's in a big hurry to get out!" smirked the Tesco delivery man.

"My wife... she suffers with dementia and has to be isolated whenever we have visitors," Reg said calmly.

Libby kicked the door with her bare foot repeatedly until her big toe throbbed and began oozing blood. A crack appeared in the bottom door panel... how she wished she could crawl through it like Alice. She clawed at the paintwork as the walls began moving in, her heart racing and thumping against her ribs like an alien. She began flinging her body against the door.

"She's a danger to herself, I'm afraid," Reg sighed, as he unpacked the last shopping bag.

Blind with terror and tears, Libby's entire body turned to ice as she liquefied to the floor in a giant yawn, like Munch's painting.

The linoleum floor was sticking to her face when she woke. Cassie's rough wet tongue licked at her hand. She tried to turn over, but her body wouldn't respond.

"Look what you've done to yourself again," Reg said, rolling her onto her back and placing a cold damp towel across her forehead; she threw it off.

"Why, Reg?" she whispered, the words tasting sour in her mouth. "Why did you lock me in again, when you know I'm claustrophobic?"

To protect you dear; I don't want you to go into hospital again."

Libby stared at the ceiling. "At least I'd be out of this prison."

"But this is our home," Reg said sheepishly.

"No, it's not! You won't even let me go into the garden!" she said, struggling to raise her aching head.

Reg hobbled off in the direction of the kitchen.

In her mind's eye Libby envisaged the wide-open spaces she pined for: green fields flowing gently with wheat and Cassie running with ears flapping, her head popping up above unfurling sheaths. She loved the boundless festoons of cloud which painted images in the sky. She pictured the sharp hawthorn briars, naked in winter's bleakness, neatly manicured by weary tractors; and the haunting ancient beech shivering in shaded forests.

"You remember our walks, don't you Cassie?" Libby sighed. "Think yourself lucky… at least you have a dog flap."

The dog's soft brown eyes gazed back knowingly into hers.

"Take your tablets now Libby," Reg said briskly, handing her a glass of water. "Then you must rest while I get supper."

Libby always did as he asked; he'd given up a good job in insurance to look after her. He'd even had to pull his front tooth out because they couldn't afford a dentist. As she heaved herself to standing, she caught sight of herself in the mirror. Her once ebony curtain of hair was streaked with dramatic bands of white and her olive skin had paled into sickly ashen. Despite feeling guilty to have wounded him with her words, she decided to flush the tablets down the toilet.

"Why *can't* I tend the garden, Reg?" Libby asked gently, lifting the heavy muslin curtain from the cloudy window to peer out. Despite the gardener's regular visits, it looked a shambles. "I'd make a much better job of it… and Cassie and I could play with a ball outside."

"You know it's a bad idea… imagine if you had one of your dizzy spells and fell over again. You'd have to go to hospital!"

Sometimes their beautiful old garden came to life in her dreams. It was a magical place with a huge variety of mature trees and plenty of grass for Cassie to run. But they'd had to move when Reg gave up his job.

Libby and Cassie solemnly followed Reg into the cluttered sitting room. Libby plucked a photograph from the dresser and wiped off a misty film of dust with her index finger. It was their daughter Jenny. She remembered the day the picture was taken. She'd been their only child, long awaited and a joyous surprise as she'd thought the menopause had arrived. She could remember watching Jenny's ballet classes and was so proud when she got a place at the Royal Academy. But after that, Libby's memories of her daughter had become grey and faded.

Whenever Jenny visited these days she didn't look like their daughter at all. She spent all her time chatting to Reg and didn't seem interested in Libby. She'd try to hear their conversation, but they mostly spoke in whispers. Jenny would look up sharply if Libby stood up or spoke. She felt sad and left out. Perhaps she'd bake a cake next time Jenny came… although Reg wouldn't allow her to cook anymore.

Among her best memories were the times when she and Reg would sit on a park bench after Cassie's evening walk; they'd hold hands to watch the shaping of the night and the eerie moon shadows. They'd identify the constellations that rule the twilight sky, occasionally spotting a shooting star. Reg said they were just pieces of dust entering the earth's atmosphere, but Libby believed they were wishing stars. She was sad that Reg said it was too dangerous to go out these days, especially at night. Her dreams and nightmares were now deeply entwined with her memories... they were all just shadowlands to her.

One day Libby had escaped whilst Reg was putting the bin out. She had no time to grab her coat, so she just took a chance. It was winter, and the ground was hard and cold as iron beneath her bare feet. Over the road, she discovered a narrow footpath leading down towards a Church and beyond that she could see open fields with acres of sky. The old metal gate groaned as she entered the cemetery and gazed up at the pretty church. The meadows beckoned her; she was just about to go on, when a strange feeling of sorrow enveloped her. The feeling seemed familiar somehow and suddenly caused her excruciating pain. She began to tremble and shiver, feeling sure she needed to find something in that place... something that she'd lost a long time ago. Libby struggled clumsily across the slippery grass mounds, reading names from the tombstones aloud; some were obscured by lichen and others had engraving so fresh, she thought she could feel the spirits beneath her. She began weeping for no apparent reason, her chest heaving under some heavy weight.

"Are you alright?" shouted a plump blonde woman. "You're Elizabeth Brown, aren't you?"

"I... I," Libby began. "Yes, I am."

Soon she was strapped into the Community Warden's

van and before she knew it, found herself back inside the bungalow. Libby stood rigid inside the door like a porcelain statue.

"Oh, thank God you're alright," Reg had said, giving her a hug.

Since then, every day was the same. Every night since her escape, she would lay awake, tormented by the strange feeling at the churchyard.

The morning after the Tesco delivery, Libby examined herself carefully in her dressing table mirror, poking at the pouches beneath her eyes and examining the numerous wrinkles she'd not noticed before. No wonder her daughter didn't want to speak with her... she looked a mess.

In the drawer, she found the hairclip that Jenny bought her on Mothering Sunday when she was fifteen; it was a silver shooting star, glittering with tiny crystals. She brushed her hair thoughtfully and then twisted it up, pinning it like she used to. She took out a dress from her wardrobe; it was deep blue with a glittery hemline. It fitted well but revealed the many bruises across her chest and shoulders from the impact with the door.

"Is Jenny visiting today, Reg?" she asked cheerily as she entered the kitchen, hoping for a compliment from him.

"No, not today," he said without bothering to look up.

"When will she be coming again?" Libby asked.

Reg tutted, then glanced her up and down in a dissatisfied way. "She's on holiday for two weeks... and I think you need a cardigan over that."

"Oh," said Libby.

Cassie was curled up on her favourite old worn sofa; Libby sat beside her, stroking her head gently. She whispered to the dog that they would escape together one day soon; this time she wouldn't bother with the churchyard – they'd head straight out into the open countryside.

When that opportunity came, it all happened very fast. It was early morning whilst the postman was carrying in a parcel of Cassie's dog food for Reg. Libby and Cassie slipped silently through the front door; her in her carpet slippers and the dog without a lead or collar. No one saw them leave, and as far as Reg knew she was still in her bedroom.

Now the path was overgrown with summer grasses... flaxen maiden-hair and soft rose-tinged meadow grass. White lace cow parsley, their giant heads made from hundreds of tiny snowflake flowers, swayed in the breeze. Pink blackberry flowers lined the hedgerows and Libby spied some tiny wild strawberries hiding low, which she picked and shared with Cassie. The sun beat down and Libby raised her face to smile at the sky, allowing the fresh air to rush into her lungs. Aeroplane trails bled into fine ribs and crossed each other into a kiss. Cassie started running in the wheat which was turning golden; she seemed much slower than Libby remembered. It was the shrillness of the birdsong that took Libby most by surprise; she only heard a muffled blur through the double glazing at the bungalow.

In the distance, a windmill perched like a glittering birthday candle on a golden hill. In the shadow of the undulating Downs, Libby and Cassie wandered through field after field until they reached a fallow clover pasture dotted with scarlet poppies. Cassie rolled over and over whilst Libby stood with her arms out-stretched, screaming with joy at the top of her voice.

Suddenly the sky seemed to darken, and gloomy platoons of cloud began to hasten across the sky towards them. She thought of Reg. She felt sad that he wasn't there to enjoy this wonderful place with her. She called Cassie and they retraced their steps back to the churchyard. As the old gate creaked, Libby paused briefly in the hope she'd remember what had caused her such pain before; but nothing came.

As they crossed the road to the bungalow she noticed the front door gaping wide open. Reg was sitting on the door step with his head buried in his hands, his bald patch polished into a shine in the sun. She called his name and he looked up with eyes clouded in tears; his whole body was shaking. He gave a brief toothless smile and then slumped backwards, clutching his chest.

"Reg!" Libby shouted.

With tears stinging her eyes, she rolled him onto his left side into the recovery position. She dashed inside the bungalow, quickly scanning the sitting room for the telephone. She'd recently seen Reg talking on it in the far corner of the room. She dialled 999 and spoke clearly; her husband was suffering from a seizure she thought; but no, she didn't know exactly where they lived. Telling them to hold on, she dropped the phone to the floor and dashed to the neighbour's house. She begged the lady to go in and give the ambulance directions. Returning to Reg, she found he was pallid and grey; he'd stopped breathing. All at once her CPR training came back to her and she began working on Reg's limp body. By the time the paramedics arrived, Reg had regained his colour and was breathing again, albeit erratically.

As Reg was being loaded into the ambulance, he smiled and blew Libby a kiss. She was just about to get into the vehicle with him when the GP, who visited occasionally to talk with Reg, drove up with Jenny sitting beside him.

"We'll take you to the hospital, Libby," shouted Jenny. "But first Doctor Peters would like to have a quick chat with you in the house… is that OK?"

Libby nodded, and they went inside. The sweat was pouring off her. She sat beside Cassie, who was curled up on the old sofa; she allowed tears of relief to flow down her face.

"It's all my fault," she sobbed. "Cassie and I ran away, and poor Reg must have been out looking everywhere for us."

"Oh, I doubt he'd be able to do that, Mrs. Brown," said the doctor. "It was probably as much as he could do to sit in the doorway."

"I feel so ungrateful," Libby went on. "He's such a good man; he had to give us his job because of my dementia."

"My dear Mrs. Brown, you have not been diagnosed with dementia," Doctor Peters said, walking over to pat her knee gently. "Reg is a sick man... he is suffering from a very severe form of agoraphobia."

"He couldn't even go out to get his tooth fixed, which is why he pulled it out himself," Jenny added.

Libby was dumbfounded.

"But Doctor Peters, how is it then that I don't recognise my own daughter anymore?" she asked, pointing at Jenny.

"Oh no... I'm not your daughter Libby! I'm Reg's care worker, Yvonne; we agreed it would be better... kinder... for you to think I was Jenny." She paused momentarily. "You've never been able to accept Jenny's death, have you?"

"Her death?" Libby asked in a wobbly voice.

"Yes," said Doctor Peters. "I'm sorry to have to remind you Mrs. Brown... but your daughter died four years ago, in a road traffic accident. You suffered a break-down and were sent temporarily to a sanatorium. Reg had resigned from his job already because of his illness and, by downsizing your house, you've both been managing to look after each other."

Suddenly it all became clear to Libby.

"Reg thought it best for you to believe I was Jenny until

you were stronger, but it just continued on; there were many times I tried to persuade Reg to be open with you."

At last she could allow all those painful memories to come flooding back. She cried on Yvonne's shoulders for many hours before getting ready to visit Reg in the hospital.

Stag Night

She was frocked in innocence with long stilettoed legs. The predators watched her turn her graceful neck, head tilted to listen to a song. The light caught in her vanilla hair and her purity drew us in. Sad globes adorned with long lashes flickered, unaware that we watched. Every man there wished he could strip her naked and keep her to himself.

Suddenly she sprang into an evocative dance, shifting from side to side. The turmoil of her moves amplified the intense craving of her audience.

I didn't pursue her but called my dog, un-cocked my gun, and walked home.

The Girl on the Bridge

The snow fell silently throughout the frosty December night, lazily drifting and dancing across the open skies over the south downs and quietly encapsulating the beech wood at Eartham into a magical frozen tomb. Tucked between Stoke Down and Bow Hill, the magnificent twisted shapes of the ancient yews at Kingley Vale rose steadfast above the forest. Continuous snow deposits on the spreading branches of these giant watchers embellished them into beautiful Christmas trees, like those still adorning most Sussex homes. Nestled beneath its fairy-tale castle, the picturesque medieval town of Arundel resembled the finest of many festive greeting cards still hanging in hallways. Ponds and puddles were glued with thick layers of ice, but the virulent river Arun still flowed freely, dark and hidden secretly beneath a sparkling sheet of bewitched glass.

From the bedroom window of her Tudor town house, Grace pressed her little turned up nose between the diamond shapes of leaded glass, peering down at the snow-covered streets below. She ran excitedly downstairs to ask if Christmas had returned; her mother told her that January always brought the snow, but she'd need to wait almost another year before Christmas returned.

After an eagerly devoured breakfast, the petite little girl in the bright pea-green coat rushed merrily ahead of her father with her long hair shimmering down her back in a swaying blonde curtain. Trundling along after her, Peter's shouts became brasher and more urgent, splintering the icy air; she didn't seem to hear him. Eventually she paused, turning back to wave her little woolly mittens at him with a beaming smile; a smile he would treasure for the rest of his life.

"Take my picture here, Daddy," Grace giggled as she

wiped a fresh layer of snow off the wall of the old stone bridge.

"OK, but stop right there," he agreed breathlessly, trying to catch up.

Peter whispered a curse as he realised the camera screen had frozen and began shaking it vigorously, breathing on the lens to bring it back to life. He stared through the viewfinder of his old Pentax at the cute little seven-year-old with a golden fringe peeping like a pelmet from beneath her winter bonnet; it would make any father smile he thought. Peter soon became puzzled; there appeared to be a gathering of weird dark clouds hovering just above his daughter's head, looming over her like a coven of menacing phantoms. As if by premonition, something made him look up from the camera and to his horror, Grace stood on top of the bridge wall... teetering on the edge but still giggling.

It all seemed to happen in slow motion. Still wearing her endearing smile, the child tipped sideways, her right foot daintily poised on the wall and her left foot suspended in a ballerina balance. All at once, the little red snow-boot left the wall and Grace disappeared below.

Nightmares had tortured Peter every night since, cruelly taking that agonising moment a step further. He imagines the G-force wobbling her rosy apple cheeks into an exaggerated smile as she fell; her bonnet loosening and flying off, leaving her long blonde hair quivering high above her like a cat's tail. In his dreams, day or night, he recurrently hears the sound of the brittle ice sheet cracking as she entered the water with the grace of a beautiful sea bird.

Without giving it a second thought, Peter had scrambled over the edge of the bridge after Grace and ejected himself down like Superman, breaking the ice beside the hole she had disappeared through like Alice's white rabbit. He

53

didn't feel the ice-cold water until it closed above his head, immediately muting the sounds of the outside world. He realised he had entered a muffled, silent world, which took possession of any living creature entering its depths; the river had engulfed them both in its surreal and unforgiving grasp.

Peter scrutinised every murky shadow through the colourless silt, distracted by tiny glittery fish darting between hair like strands of menacing weed which swayed in a curtain to hide Grace's face from him. In panic, he jerked violently through the ice-cold water, his inaudible cries releasing bubbles towards the surface. Grace eventually rose up serenely from the depths below him; her pale fragile face bloated, with fish like ice-blue eyes fixed wide and gazing emptily into the distance.

Dragging her lifeless body to the surface like a diver clutching a priceless pearl, he had thrust her head above the water like a marker buoy. She didn't gasp for air as he did, but instead her body floated limply on the surface beside him like a spectre.

Peter had journeyed in a zombie like state over Stopham bridge every working day since the accident, barely conscious of the weather or the season. He was never aware of the sparkling pear-shaped raindrops suspended on bare trees, or the sun cracking a smile through the clouds; nor the wind tugging at his raincoat. He never heard the small bird heralding the sun's rise as stars faded and the black velvet sky gradually paled into morning. He was oblivious to everyone and every living thing around him. He detested this cold-hearted fourteenth century stone link which spanned the river Arun, its six mighty arches speckled with hundreds of years of gull droppings. Weeds grew virulently in the cracks against decaying stone, infested with an eczema of lichen. He wished it would crumble away completely and fall crashing into the river, soon to be consumed by the sea forever. Peter often pondered on how many lives it had taken over the years, feeling certain that one day he would quietly, and thankfully, slip over the side and disappear forever.

Since the middle-ages, the little town of Arundel had scarcely changed. It consisted of a variety of Tudor beamed and Georgian buildings housing innumerable antique shops and boutiques; no major multiple shops sold their wares here, apart from the usual chains of Italian restaurants. There were plenty of cafes and restaurants... any type, any kind. Peter had occasionally decided to stop at one of the quaint little tea shops for a fragrant jasmine tea on his lonely way home after work; but he knew that no amount of company could ever ease the pain in his empty heart.

It was a bitterly cold Friday and the river flowed swift and deep today, the current preventing many small fishing boats from mooring. Even in the summer, its treacherous swell had caught many families of picnickers by surprise as they wrestled with ropes to reach the shoreline. Countless dogs caught in the untrustworthy flow had ended their lives there, despite their frenzied struggles. Peter glanced up at the medieval castle, dramatically erupting from the hillside to hover majestically over the quaint little town below. It always reminded him of reading to Grace her favourite bedtime story, where Rapunzel drapes her long hair from a tower and is rescued by a handsome prince. Peter's tiny shop stood in the castle's shadow, making the many dark days of winter seem like an endless entombment. For most of his life he had made and sold jewellery to what he considered to be very spoilt, pernickety, menopausal females; they would swoop in like magpies whenever he placed something new and sparkly in the window. In the past, he had enjoyed carving his own designs, but his creations became more sporadic when his eyesight deteriorated, and arthritis began twisting and distorting his fingers.

Ten years had tumbled away to this very day since the river had stolen his daughter. There was to be a candlelit service in the Roman Catholic cathedral which dominated the skyline alongside the castle. Peter struggled through the day in a fog of dark thoughts until four o'clock arrived. The prospect of snow had deterred many visitors to the town, so he locked up early. Tentatively, Peter made his way to the nearby grand house of worship, steeped in history and built from Bath stone in a French gothic style. The impressive Cathedral Church of our Lady and St. Philip Howard perched precariously on the west bank of the river as the valley opens out into the coastal plain. He was greeted by the imposing carved cedar doors at the west wing, which were gnarled and ravenous for oil. Glancing up at an arch of uninviting gargoyles framing the entrance, he shivered and entered the magnificent edifice apprehensively. The swelling audience mumbled quietly, echoing his own melancholia throughout the cold stone arches of the building. Peter felt his leg twitching nervously when he noticed his ex-wife, Dorothy, sitting a few rows ahead with her new husband; her love had so quickly turned into a mask of hate for him after the accident. But he couldn't blame her for that; he knew she could never forgive him for losing their only daughter.

Eventually the lights dimmed; candles flickered and reflected in the numerous stained-glass windows, especially the beautifully coloured rose window just ahead of him. The purity of the choir voices seemed to soothe him for a time, but before long the music shaped an unswallowable lump in Peter's throat. Tears began to fill his eyes as the beautiful flutist, with her golden fringe framing her sparkling ice-blue eyes like a pelmet, began to play. It was like an intoxicating perfume which mesmerised the whole of her audience. He tried to imagine what Grace might look like now, but he could only ever see her as she was that day on the bridge. Suddenly overflowing with emotion, he became desperate to escape. Whispering apologies as he went, Peter struggled clumsily to the end of the row and fled out into the ice-bound street.

In the shadow of a nearby streetlight, Peter's solitary figure paused in the centre of Stopham Bridge. A mist was rising from the chill of the water below. He draped his aching arms over the edge, allowing his head to dangle loose and low, with gravity draining blood to his head, his feet lightening from the ground. Flakes of snow began lazily floating down over him, hovering like goose feathers around his head and quickly covering him in a white sheet.

He had always refused to believe in the existence of angels, but at that moment little Grace appeared beside him, with an array of snowflakes mingling like diamonds into her long blonde hair.

"Dad…" she said. "Thank you for coming."

She giggled as her cold hand slipped into his and their shadows dissolved slowly into the mist.

The Dandelion Bed

*Some see it as a pest and weed, but the dandelion is a gift
to a loved one as a promise of total faithfulness, forever.*

As her car pulled up at the Old Rectory, the Wisteria
tangled frontage hadn't changed since she was a child.

Tentatively she approached the huge wooden door
which towered above her, gnarled and thirsty for paint. She
struggled with the old lock, leaning all her weight on the
door until it groaned open. Vaguely aware of it closing
behind her, Alison stood mesmerised, listening to the
creaking house. She pictured her mother rushing out from
the kitchen wearing a floral apron, her cheeks red from the
heat of the stove. She remembered her brother, Matthew,
careering down the lengthy mahogany banister in a
pillowcase at Christmas, and the tall bauble infested fir tree
reaching way up to the gallery. As she used to drift off to
bed she'd joyfully pat the angel at the top of the tree, hoping
she'd smile back at her.

Matthew had persuaded her to come and stay at the
house; she must supervise the redecoration ready for sale,
to pay for their mother's care home fees. She'd pleaded
with him that it would be the worst possible place for her to
be, but then her own house had become an empty shrine
over the past fourteen months since John died.

There was a muffled barking from outside... she'd
forgotten the dog was in the car. Despite her years, the hefty
Labrador jumped agilely down and ran excitedly to the
front door wagging her tail eagerly. Once inside she began
sniffing enthusiastically and as Alison opened the sitting
room door, Millie rushed in. The room hadn't changed
much in over thirty years; time seemed to have stood still.
She caressed the soft puce velvet drapes which now looked
so faded and sad, whereas the old brown leather

Chesterfields seemed to have improved with age. She patted her father's sturdy walnut writing desk, picturing him there peering through his horn-rimmed spectacles at one of his sketches. She was glad to see his collection of water colours still hanging proudly above the fire place, now somewhat washed-out by fire ash and time. The dust covered chandelier was missing several baubles and a delicate layer of powder had formed a white lace cloth on top of the maple coffee table.

The dog trotted behind Alison through the hallway into the large but very ancient kitchen, where her mother always spent many hours slaving over the range. Wiping the grime from the kitchen window, she could see that the gardener had recently scythed the lawn into a long shag-pile carpet. As the ancient plumbing rebelled against the filling of the kettle, Millie sighed and flopped at Alison's feet.

"Don't tell me... I forgot your breakfast *again!*" Alison said apologetically.

Whilst Alison rummaged through unpacked bags for bowls and biscuits, Millie began to growl beside the back door. The door wouldn't budge at first, so Alison had to fiddle with the lock for some time before it finally flung open.

"Is that you, Deeds?" she called out.

The door of the woodshed flapped vacantly open and closed. Ignoring her food, the dog stormed out with hackles raised and stood peering warily inside the shed, with a front paw raised. Feeling a shiver, Alison approached cautiously. A foul odour hit her, forcing her to quickly cover her face. She could see no evidence of what might cause the hideous smell; just a small pile of logs in the corner and a few old sacks scattered about the floor.

"Alright Millie, let's go and explore," Alison chirped, slamming the shed door firmly shut.

A weak sun yawned through the February greyness. A cheeky robin on a pitchfork beside a mound of limp weeds brought her attention to the small signs of regeneration in the garden. She strolled across the ragged lawn, admiring how Deeds had begun pruning all the shrubs; his attention to detail hadn't slackened over the years. She stepped through the flint archway into the secret garden; in the summer months it was a magical world of vigorous rose briars, sweet jasmine, honeysuckle and giant hydrangeas. The poor dandelions were merely an untidy bed of weed now, but soon it would be spread with bright golden flower heads. She had many fond memories of helping her father pick them for making his homemade wine.

"Always leave one flower for each you pick, then you'll have seed heads for the summer," he'd told her; and with a smile he added, "If you blow on a white dandelion and every seed scatters, you know you are truly loved."

Later in the year the cotton candy spheres would create a magical moonscape for Alison as a child, overflowing with delicate white baubles. Counting the stars before blowing them, she'd sit entranced, watching them float away on the breeze. The dandelion bed eventually became her and John's favourite place; they'd escaped there during their engagement party, returning with the white candyfloss seeds in their hair. "I'll always be here for you, little Ali, you know that," he'd promised. She closed her eyes, remembering how good it felt to be wrapped in his strong arms, and to be loved and cared for. "I'll meet you here…" he would whisper.

"It's cold, Mills," Alison said, shivering. "Let's go back in."

As they approached the house, a large wood-pigeon lay injured on the patio beside the French windows. Millie carefully inspected it and lifted a front paw.

"Necks probably broken," rasped a voice from behind them.

Millie's hackles rose immediately at the sight of the scruffy bulk of a man; unshaven, with lank mousey hair.

"Jacob Jones," he said, wiping his grubby hand on his trousers and extending it to her.

"Alison McKenzie. You must be my brother's builder... but I thought you had a key?"

"Oh, but I do," he grinned, flashing a small brass object. He grabbed the wounded bird and wrung its neck before tossing it into the hedgerow. "Never was keen on those vermin."

Alison gasped, feeling shocked by this harshness. Glancing down at his muddy boots, she suggested he enter the house through the kitchen. He didn't offer to remove the boots but instead wandered on into the sitting room.

"Interesting display of paintings you got 'ere," he scoffed.

Alison stopped in her tracks, staring in disbelief; all the paintings were tilted to one side... something her father had often done to warn if Mother was in a bad mood, or if a dentist's appointment was imminent. John had adopted this same practise over the years, like the time he lost his job; and then when his cancer was first diagnosed.

"This is the main room for redecoration," Alison said, trying to conceal her astonishment.

"Looks like it'll be needing a bit more than a lick of paint, ma'am," Jones said.

"Well, it's only to get the place on the market," she responded curtly. "I'm staying in the guest wing, so I'd prefer if you to do that last."

"Course; I wouldn't wanna go disturbing your rest, now would I? I'll be 'ere tomorrow at nine then."

"Fine," Alison answered lamely.

"I'll be letting meself out now," he said.

As she heard the door slam, her phone rang.

"Ali?" said a familiar voice.

"Hi Matt; I've just been talking to your builder bloke. Odd character… eyes very close together," she said as she walked around adjusting all the paintings to level positions again.

Matthew laughed. "He's a good chap really; bit difficult to understand perhaps, but salt of the earth nevertheless. He must have got back from Ireland early. How are things going there?"

"He's starting work tomorrow."

"No, I meant how are *you* doing?"

"Oh, just more memories to deal with, thank you; or should I say, different ones," she said flatly.

"Why don't you go and revisit some of our childhood haunts… see how the landscape's changed and get some fresh air," Matthew suggested. "By the way, I'm sorry but you may have to stay an extra day or two as the original schedule of work didn't include refurbishing the outbuildings."

Alison felt she was being taken advantage of, but she knew the wisdom of her brother's words; she needed country air and a new mindset. She didn't want to mention the lopsided paintings to her brother, but she felt spooked and very weary.

After making an omelette and drinking a large glass of red wine, she retired to the guest wing with Millie where she and John had often stayed. It felt strange sleeping in there without him. Throughout his illness she'd lain awake at night listening for any faltering in his breath; she was devastated they'd had so little time together after the diagnosis. Once in the hospice he became so thin and frail that only his eyes were still recognisable. Now she lay awake each night, tormented by missed opportunities to tell him how much she loved him.

As dawn made a fugitive of the night, Alison was relieved to see the sunlight illuminating the bedroom curtains. She gazed down from the window at a fluffy blanket of snow which muffled the place in a unique type of deafness. She ate an early breakfast in an attempt to avoid the builders and togged herself up in her warmest coat and boots. Outside flakes of snow floated lazily over the gardens, creating an exquisite and magical world of white. She glanced in through the archway where the secret garden and dandelion bed had become ethereal.

Panting clouds, Millie led the way through the garden gate and out along a slippery path towards wonderful views of the icy South Downs. The sky was blue with high white cloud layering across it in ribs. Tall firs crested by the recent snowfall stood on the horizon like attentive choir boys whereas others hid, naked as brooms, in the cloak of winter. The dog suddenly dashed down the bank into an ice-covered pond over which Matthew had once constructed a rope swing between two large oaks. Many summers ago, she and John had sat there with a picnic lunch and after some wine both decided to paddle; how she'd screamed at the leeches whilst John calmly and gently removed them from her legs one by one. *Why did John break his promise... why did he leave her?* If only she could go too; if only she could have sucked his disease into her own body and synchronised their death. Life was completely futile without him.

In an attempt to blot out negative thoughts, Alison began to swing her arms briskly and draw in deep lungsful of cold air. It was good to embrace the freshness and feel blood rushing through her veins once more. They walked for what seemed like hours until the motorway cut a huge grey sash through their green carpet. Her legs had begun to ache and even the dog had slowed her pace.

"I suppose we really should go and supervise," Alison sighed, patting Millie's head. The dog gazed back at her with tender seal brown eyes.

In the distance, the Old Rectory looked like a beautiful antique Christmas card. She paused to admire it, but then Millie unexpectedly let out a single bark and her hackles rose as though she sensed something was wrong.

When they reached the house, it was deserted with no sign of any tradesmen. Alison filled a bowl of water for the dog and decided to try to locate the whereabouts of Deeds. As she headed towards the secret garden, her phone jingled in her pocket.

"Ali, are you there?"

"Yes, Matt."

"Something's not right there," he said. She could sense panic in his voice.

"What do you mean?"

"Peter phoned from Ireland... his transport broke down and they won't be able to start work until next week."

"Next week," Alison repeated. "But I don't understand."

"It's not..." The phone signal suddenly died.

Alison was trying to call Matthew back when something cold and metallic hit her hard in the left side of her head. Scull vibrating, she crumpled to the floor, her face plummeting into the dandelion bed. She was aware of something thick and moist oozing from her left ear and then she blacked out.

When she came to, she was lying on her back half naked and staring up into a stone sky. Suddenly a huge weight landed upon her. The smell of stale sweat assaulted her nostrils and a pair of rat like eyes aligned with hers.

"You look like a lonely lady who needs some loving!" the gruff voice said.

"NO!" she gurgled, suppressing vomit rising to her throat. She struggled but couldn't move. Then she heard a whistle… it was John's signature whistle; the one that he alone could ever do. Furious barking erupted and approached rapidly, followed by a menacing growling beside her.

"Get off me you mutt!" the man shouted, kicking out his leg.

Alison felt the impact of the pitchfork in the man's back. His mouth gaped goldfish like and then his body slumped across her like a corpse.

"Are you alright, Miss Alison?" asked a familiar voice.

"I… I don't know," she wheezed. "Can you get him off me, Deeds?"

She felt the fork jerk from the immobile body, causing a small gasp of foul breath to escape from his mouth as he flopped to one side of her.

"Is he dead?" she asked.

"No, I don't think so, Miss, but it would be wise to call the police straight away."

At that point, she blacked out again.

Alison woke to find Deeds wrapping his jacket around her. "You've had a shock, Miss. Let me take you inside," he said, mopping the blood from her head with a white handkerchief.

She felt like a small child as she stared over Deeds' shoulder at Millie's stock-still shape guarding the huge motionless heap in the dandelion bed.

"Thank you, Deeds," Alison said as he laid her on the sofa.

"Drink this Miss," he instructed, handing her a glass. "It's lucky I decided to spend an extra day here in the greenhouse on those geraniums!"

The liquid glided down her throat leaving a warm

burning sensation. She gazed up at the wall ahead; once again her father's paintings were all tilted to one side. She began to shiver and shake, and Deeds clumsily piled a big blanket over her. Millie rushed into the room and pushed her head into Alison's lap. A policeman appeared behind her.

"Paramedics have just arrived to deal with your injuries and check you over Mrs. McKenzie. We've been looking for this man for several weeks. He absconded from The Vale Psychiatric Institute a month ago and it looks as though he's been sleeping rough in your wood shed. I'll come back shortly to take some details from you if I may."

Alison nodded perplexedly.

"I'll stay with her," said Deeds as he topped up the brandy in Alison's glass.

"Your whistle, Deeds… it's so similar to my John's whistle," she said before taking another sip.

"What me, Miss Alison? Oh, no, I'm afraid my whistling days are over… I haven't been able to whistle since my dentures were fitted five years ago."

The Day Sussex Died

Saddled to the back of a coveted southern coastline, which over the centuries many had given their lives to defend, the South Downs smouldered in ochre and russet. We'd wandered far across many meadows until the motorway tore a huge sash through our green carpet. Above us the scared sky was littered with white baubles of fluffy cloud, hung with large birds floating like kites.

The dogs submerged themselves into an ethereal pool flanked by tall evergreens, standing by like attentive choirboys. Shadows lengthened, and the landscape blended into sepia. As we cut across ploughed fields carved with cavernous trenches, the sun began to slip in a magnificent fiery finale on top of trees dripping scarlet leaves in constant flows of arterial blood. Twilight was drawing in. Ahead of us a crooked figure materialised, carefully pioneering the track and dragging one leg.

"Like you, I've left it a little late to return to barracks," observed the elderly man.

The sun suddenly fell below the horizon and we were enveloped in the grey cloak of dusk; the landscape no longer welcomed us. I wanted to get past him, but the man began a conversation. Before long I was listening to his life story and how he'd been an orphan raised by a cruel aunt.

"I lied about my age to join Kitchener's Army, but army food was a big improvement on potato peelings!" he said, expanding his pigeon coloured moustache into a lopsided grin. His cheeks were flushed with exertion, his nose resembled an old potato, but he had kind eyes.

I sensed a deep sadness in this man; this man called Victor. I listened tolerantly for as long as I could bear about how he travelled all over the world with the Royal Sussex Regiment.

"I've travelled by tank, rickshaw and sampan," he said. "But sadly, I've never flown."

I was quite relieved when we reached Saxon Meadow where I lived with my parents in a small scruffy cottage with too many pets. Victor saluted me before crossing the road to The Meadows Retirement home.

I bumped into Victor many times that autumn; mainly because he had a habit of blocking the path. We'd walk along for a while together until the dogs lost their patience with the pace and ran on ahead. I began to enjoy his stories and soon found myself being drawn into the past.

I'd never known my own grandparents and had always detested history lessons at school; but I found myself researching some of the stories Victor told me. I discovered that the Southdowners were men from all across Sussex... Victor must have been the youngest in the Battalions at the Boar's Head in Richebourg-l'Avoue, northern France. On the 30th June 1916 the battle lasted less than five hours but seventeen officers, hundreds of men and over a thousand were killed, wounded or captured. What was supposed to be a diversion from the Battle of the Somme, turned into a massacre because the German Army was waiting for them.

Despite him telling me he'd had a wonderful life with his wife, Elspeth, and their three daughters, I suspected there was something Victor wasn't telling me.

Winter deepened its grip and the meadows darkened early. Late one afternoon I found myself engulfed in a fog which prowled around naked trees scaring the birds into silence. I was alone on a desolate and colourless landscape. It felt like the gloomy land of despair that Victor had described. I was taken aback when he suddenly emerged in the foreground sitting awkwardly on a tree stump, leaning on his stick. He was staring into the mist, with eyes afire.

"Twelfth battalion went over the top; but we found the Hun waiting for us," he cursed into the fog.

"Hi Victor, are you OK?" I asked as I approached. He didn't respond, but kept searching into the vapours, as though he could see things hidden in the mist.

"*Heavy fire ahead... fix bayonets!*" he ordered hoarsely, animating with the help of his walking stick.

"Victor... are you alright?" I repeated loudly. The dogs sat quietly like sentinels beside me.

He paused and turned to me. "It was like a butcher's shop," he muttered, with half-moons of tears welling and glistening in his eyes. "But we fought on, legs deep in corpses robbed of breath, all strewn and crumpled into mother earth. The ground shuddered, and gunfire cracked in continuous blasts. Every man's face was distorted in a fearful grimace, smeared with blood and filth."

He paused for some while, still searching the fog. "Have you ever heard a man scream?" he barked at me.

I shook my head mutely, noticing his hands trembling.

"That mortifying sound will haunt a man all his days... nothing compares with it." He paused, and a cheeky twinkle returned to the old man's eyes. "Not even my Elspeth in labour!"

The fog was lifting, and I pointed to one of the dogs rolling in fox muck; we both laughed, agreeing that a dog should be allowed to be a dog. As we continued on together, I noticed his thoughts seemed to darken again.

"I was hit in the leg by a shell and couldn't move," he said grasping his right leg as though it had just happened. "Artillery fire all around, I realised I was trapped in 'no man's land'... I felt sure it was time for me to meet my maker."

We stopped walking for a moment to allow him to catch his breath.

"But I found myself being carried on a soldier's back as he staggered across the chaos of the battle field, splashing in rusty pools of blood; our own trenches had been obliterated."

"Someone saved your life?" I asked.

"Within seconds of bringing me back I looked up to thank him... his whole chest exploded into my face." Victor stood pale like a waxen statue. "I can still smell the iron of his blood; it went all over me. He was a true hero. Blunden wrote that it was 'The Day Sussex Died'... well, something died in me that day, young as I was."

"You were a hero as well, Victor," I said. But he just shook his head.

"This is my stop," he said as we arrived at Saxon Meadow. "Will you be all right on your own from here, my dear?"

"Don't worry, Victor; as I've told you before, I only live around the corner from here."

A few months passed until I next saw Victor. It was April and he was sitting on a stile, gazing across a young wheat field, whispering into an invisible passage of wind.

"I'm waiting for the poppies to reappear," he said, twitching his grey moustache at me. I noticed his hair had thinned to opalescence.

We both looked to the horizon where the South Downs wore a fresh dappled green cloak.

"You know I tried to make the most of his sacrifice for me," he sighed as he looked directly into my eyes.

I sat down on the grass beside him. "You mean the man who saved your life?"

"Yes. I became a CSM like him and trained young men to go to war. I had to bully and humiliate them to the point where they could fight... I mean *really* fight... and more importantly, to survive."

"That's very worthy, Victor."

"Is it, Alice? It was the least I could do. One man can't stop the machine of war; nothing can. But I constantly ask myself... was it enough?"

The dogs bolted after a rabbit and I felt compelled to follow and enjoy the countryside before the day faded.

"You're a good man, Victor," I said, placing a hand on his shoulder. "I'll see you on my way back."

"Yes, my dear... this is where I shall be."

The meadows called me on. I glanced back several times to see Victor still sitting there, wrestling with his demons.

Pussy willow adorned the hedgerows and catkins flew on the breeze. Just out of sight, I heard a lark sing.

On the way back, I felt disappointed to see the stile empty. The dogs spooked as a huge bird rose suddenly from a nearby bush, struggling to take flight. The giant wings heaved through the air as its body ascended, circling over us several times and dipping into a 'wing wave' before it finally flew off. As I watched its bulky shape disappear into the distance, I couldn't quite tell if it was an eagle or a buzzard, but somehow it seemed familiar.

Time soldiered on and, like the country saying goes, May arrived like a lion. Scarlet poppies paraded in the fields and I began to wonder how Victor was and whether he'd seen them. I found myself entering the foyer of the retirement home, having tied the dogs to the front gate.

A woman dressed in black approached me. "Can I help you?"

"Yes, I wondered if I could see Victor... Victor Baker."

She looked at me quizzically. "I'm afraid my grandfather died two months ago."

"Oh, I'm sorry, I didn't..."

71

"We have been clearing his apartment and are off to the cathedral for a memorial service in the RSR chapel. He was one of the last survivors from The Battle of the Boar's Head, you know."

As the news gradually sunk in, I found myself trying to puzzle out how I'd seen Victor sitting on the stile just a few weeks ago.

"You must be Alice," the woman said. "Grandpa was quite smitten by you; he told us about the walks you'd had together and how you were such a good listener. It's strange but he never spoke much to us family about his army days... will you join us at the Cathedral?"

"Thank you, but I need to get the dogs back to feed them." I said.

"Wait a moment, Alice," she said. "I think he would have liked you to have this."

She handed me a sepia photo of Victor who was easily recognisable by his heavy moustache but then his features were sculpted and young, without the potato nose.

"It's him training the young officers," I said, swallowing hard.

"Yes; my mother said he was renowned for stamping on his hat on the parade ground when his trainees got things wrong. Take it... we have other copies."

I carefully placed the picture in my top pocket.

Returning to the stile the next day, I sat looking at the poppies until dusk faded them into grey, in the hope the giant bird would return, but it didn't. I was grateful to have witnessed Victor's final journey.

So, before I go...
I must tell of scars on my heart
I've witnessed many battles, not won
or understood, yet I played my part

There's a place where no flowers grow
Where brambled wires mock a rose's thorns
Blood was spilled from innocents
For the devil of war hides his horns

Gunfire stifles the cries of men
Calling out for mother
Death washes them clean
The scent of souls, released

Inaudible orders shouted
Over thunderous cannon fire
to men already broken
Only their ghosts could hear

I took a shell in my thigh
Another's bravery saved me
His life was taken before
I could even thank him

I'll never know why I was spared
Surely not just to prepare
Other innocents for battle?
Perhaps just to tell this tale...
There will be no victors

The Game

The ground was crisp and white, his face, red and chapped with cold. Wrapped in his best tartan scarf, he gazed over at her. Through her dowdiness he could see an innocent beauty, which stirred something inside him.

She didn't notice him.

He carefully watched her graceful steps with her elegant head poised; then she vanished. He quickened his pace, calling out to her with instincts saying that she was the one.

Still, she didn't notice him.

There was a screech of brakes, a clumsy attempt at flight. She turned to see a myriad of tartan feathers falling.

He never knew she'd noticed him.

The Laridae Brothers

Peering down over sun scorched rooftops, the downy pair huddled together, waiting patiently and in complete silence. The warm scented Algarvian breeze pleasantly ruffled their feathers from time to time, allowing their sun-baked bodies to cool. The young gulls would sporadically shuffle aimlessly along the abyss that Mae had swooped down into before soaring upwards and disappearing into the distance. Bellies empty, they held on solemnly for her huge wings to return, feathers splayed and gleaming white.

From the very beginning Vicente felt his brother's presence beside him as they lay as eggs, snuggled in Mae's nest. He remembered the muffled sounds from their fragile opaque wombs of shell; his pounding pulse always one beat behind that of Erasmus. They'd hatched together, sharing their first glimpse of a dazzling cerulean sky which stung their fledgling eyes; they were hypnotised by the soporific eiderdown of cloud draped all about them.

Erasmus was always first at doing everything. From the earliest days of their life, his pleading cry demanded and received immediate attention; whereas Vicente's pitiful cheeps were barely audible above the Portuguese wind drafts. Vicente suspiciously scrutinised his brother as he periodically unfolded and flapped his dowdy grey wings.

A raw sound scratched the air as Mae arrived on enormous silvery arched wings, head down, with her red rimmed eyes glowing and her ochre feet extended before her. Her hooked saffron beak, outlined in blood red, carried a morsel she'd hunted – a mollusc that she'd thrown against a rock. Her fluffy tail feathers splayed and wagged as she elegantly lent forward to place a piece of food into each of her sons' mouths; it tasted of the ocean that the pair constantly watched, spellbound, in the distance. That sparkling mirror of ever changing shapes entranced the young gulls by day, and its moonlit shadows enchanted their nights. The brothers' eyes were filled with a thousand stars whilst Pai watched over them close by, huge and austere as a sculpture. Erasmus and Vicente were both feeling a strange yearning for flight, but Vicente was cautious and reluctant for change.

As summer progressed, Vicente noticed Erasmus frequently mantling his wings to test out his strength. Then suddenly embracing primal instincts one day, his brother let out a plaintive cry and dived unexpectedly down into a precipice. Between certain death and paradise, he managed to fasten onto a wind current and soared high above Vicente. Envy was quickly replaced by admiration as Vicente watched his brother's beautiful aerodynamic shape, until he returned on an awkward landing beside him.

Days followed with Erasmus recurrently taking to the air to practise and perfect his flying skills. After many shaky falls on the wind, he called out to Vicente, telling his brother of the many joys of flight and urging him to join him. Unconvinced, Vicente turned his back on his brother and remained hawkish and solitary on the rooftop; depressed and toxic with his own inadequacy. Many days passed where Vicente remained alone, marooned high on his island above a sea of white-washed villas sizzling in the heat amongst screeching sirens of crickets.

One night as the sun set, Pai alighted beside Vicente.

"My son, what you hold on to will always tie you down to the earth and you will be grounded here forever. You must be more like your brother and a take a chance… believe in yourself!"

Pai rose with a startling cry, his silhouette swiftly rising high above before disappearing into the clouds. When his brother returned, Vicente hid miserably, unwilling to share in his brother's mystical experiences. Pai's words haunted Vicente throughout the long hours of darkness.

Day after day Erasmus soared and glided eloquently with other fledglings and Vicente watched helplessly as they disappeared far out to sea to the nurseries of the gull world. He knew that Erasmus and his parents had lost all respect for him. Mae loyally continued to bring him food, but Vicente's pain exceeded all hunger as he was engulfed over and again in solitude.

On one particular day, as Erasmus was perched high and ready to alight from the rooftop, Vicente's intuition told him something was wrong. He pleaded with his brother to stay but Erasmus paused, gazing back at him sadly and then leapt into the skies. Vicente spent an anxious day patrolling the roof top and peering far out to the distant horizon. Angry storm clouds were moving in from North Africa and the hot and humid Sirocco wind began to howl around the rooftops. Dusky clouds began gathering together thickly overhead and all at once the twilight blackened into night.

Avo suddenly descended in a huge mantle beside Vicente.

"Your brother is lost!" screeched his grandfather. He raised his brightly coloured beak and honked loudly and plaintively up towards the black blanket of sky.

Mae and Pai searched with all the other elder gulls for days to try to find Erasmus, but he could not be found. A mighty stone fixed in Vicente's heart, becoming heavier as each day passed that his brother failed to return. He missed his brother greatly; he missed his valour and might but most of all he missed the beat of his pulse beside him in the nest each night.

One evening as Vicente sadly watched the darkening velvet sky unfold with bright heavenly bodies, he thought he could hear his brother's pulse far away in the distant ocean. He knew, even if he was able to fly, night flying was dangerous, but he allowed his feet to tip-toe right up close to the edge of the precipice. Then his beady eyes were suddenly opened to the wind streams previously invisible to him. His heart compelled him to drop, so… he let go; his body rapidly plummeted down and down. But then to his surprise, he was suddenly lifted like a leaf on a breeze as he accidentally harnessed onto a wind current. Ignoring cries from his elders on nearby rooftops, he felt the strength in his wings and began to soar.

Vicente flew further and further away from his nest; so far that he doubted he'd ever be able to return. He didn't look back, but continued heading towards that familiar pulse. Eventually the rhythm of his brother's heart seemed near. He carefully lowered to the call of the fragile beat and began descending rapidly towards the ocean, amazed that his wings held him so steady.

He was overcome with joy as he spotted Erasmus. His body was lying very still, and Vicente could see he was trapped in discarded fishing nets. Vicente managed to alight clumsily beside his brother. Ignoring the pain, he began swiping his young beak repeatedly across the nearby red rock. His sharp bill eventually obliterated the flayed covering of nets and he nestled down exhausted beside the limp feathered body of his brother… two souls again entwined with their pulses beating together in unison.

Dawn opened the Algarvian sky as the young Laridae brothers flew alongside each other towards the distant horizon, their spirits gliding and soaring together as silver angels of the skies, forever; citizens of heaven.

Drawn by the Sea

The cold metal of the wrought-iron railings imprinted hard into her back; she'd gazed for hours at the festoon of floral drapes which swamped the small wooden cross. She was reliving the final passage of the flag-draped casket as it was shouldered by stiff, awkward-walking military men. The bugles still resonated in her head, *Johnny has gone for a soldier*, as the earth engulfed the coffin.

Annie knew he wasn't here among the ancient stones encrusted with creeping yellow and brown lichen; nor was he amongst the pristine white marble standing patiently in rows. Embracing the remembrance monument with its faded ring of poppies, she hurried through the gate and fled into the street. Resisting frenzied tears, she headed towards the coast, feeling sure Johnny's spirit awaited her there with other victims of the cruel, heartless sea and its unforgiving nature.

Joining the chaos of Worthing seafront, she slipped in amongst joggers, cyclists, dog walkers, kids on scooters, and the toy train which was being bombarded by squabbling seagulls. The beach fronts of Sussex were laden with families enjoying a typical British summer with ice creams, penny arcades and all the fun of the fair, amid the underscents of greasy sun lotion. Excited children grasped onto colourful new buckets, waiting patiently as their fathers hammered windbreaks into moist recently exposed sand. All along this coastal stretch the heady smell of donuts and fish and chips blended with the undertones of the salty sea air. Annie suddenly felt nauseous.

With her long blonde hair wilting around her hunched shoulders, she walked onto the Victorian pier where Johnny and she had enjoyed their first date all those years ago. Since she was a child she'd never been drawn towards the ocean and hated the gaps between the wooden slats of the pier; but Johnny said he trusted the sea like a mother and that she should too. Often, they'd sit there on a bench holding hands to watch the fishermen, with their rugged jovial faces, haul in their catch. Tears blurred her vision as she wandered bewildered and alone with her heart dangling heavily in her chest. Snippets of conversations buzzed past her ears as people passed by wearing smells from laboratories, chatting on phones, chastising children or calling to their dogs. She did not see the frilly petticoats of tiny waves as they trickled gently towards shore; nor did she see the beauty of the twinkling ocean. She was a damaged soul, tethered and imprisoned by her grief.

Annie arrived at the busy Sea Lane café, catching sight of her pale haunted features reflected in the windows like a ghost. After many windswept walks they'd often stop here to watch the ocean and to make plans. He would give up the Navy soon he'd promised her; they'd buy a small boat where he could give sailing lessons and teach their young a true love of the ocean. Johnny was convinced they'd have big strong sons with broad shoulders like him. She walked on, wrestling with memories and unfulfilled dreams... all the life that the war had robbed them of.

Oblivious to the passing hours, she hadn't seen the beautiful crimson sunset or been aware of people slowly deserting the beach. At the end of the promenade Annie sunk down onto the shingle to gaze out across the vast sparkling ocean and the distant horizon. The sepia shadows of several vessels hung in limbo on the faded boundary between sea and sky, motionless unless she glanced away. The ocean changed its shape in a perpetual motion of dips and swells beneath the now sombre twilight sky. Dusk began to gather around her in a cloak, but she felt no urge to leave; there was nowhere she wanted to go.

She listened to the gentle 'so' of waves being sucked down, and 'ha' as they rushed back in, soothing her into a dreamlike state. Johnny's voice was calling out to her, telling her to trust the sea like a mother and join him there. Rising clumsily to her feet and stumbling towards the water, she muttered his name in whispers that were immediately snatched by the breeze. Tumbling waves now clawed at pebbles and grabbed at shells as the tide began its alluring retreat, grabbing sparkling dust down beneath each wave. The ghostly ships on the horizon beckoned persuasively to her through the canopy of the starlit sky, urging her to enter and join her sweetheart there.

She kicked off her shoes, allowing the water to lick her toes as she slowly sank into the sand in obedience to the demanding draw of the tide. She could hear Johnny's voice still calling out to her and feel his presence in the wind. Spontaneously her body launched forwards as she shouted his name into the surf which struck her brutally in the face and gurgled down her throat like liquid sandpaper. She spewed the water out and choked as the current carried her swiftly away, the swell buffeting her towards the horizon.

Annie allowed herself to drift, the waves rocking her limp body like a jellyfish on top of the water. She felt no fear; the intoxicating smell of salt reminded her of his blonde hair and coarse weathered skin. She wanted to be taken… to be sunk with Johnny's ship. She realised that she couldn't blame the sea for taking him – it was the chaos and destruction of war and the senseless weapons of man that had robbed her of him. Wherever he was… be it dark or endless night… it was where she wanted to be. She voyaged on, exposed to the elements around her and trusting that she was travelling closer to where he would be waiting for her. As the sky darkened into the ink blackness of the sea, white crests rose to play in the moonlight. Annie permitted the darkness to wrap itself around her, feeling the rise and fall of her body rocking in the swell until sleep overwhelmed her. She slept deeply; deeper than she could ever remember. She dreamt of journeys he had told her about, the wonderful places the sea had shown to him and where he'd sent her love letters from.

Something suddenly disturbed her slumbers and stirred her senses to consciousness; a queer feeling that demanded she wake up. The sky had begun to lighten but the shoreline had completely vanished. Twisting and turning in the freezing water, she could find no trace of the bottom. Icy fingers began spreading around her body like a blanket; she struggled but was unable to move from her morgue like cocoon.

Then a giant swell rose up from behind her, a wave as high as the ship that had carried Johnny away that day to the battle zone. She stared up in wonder at the tip of the surge as it bent over her floating body like a doting mother embracing her child. Taking almost human form, it cradled and nursed her, sweeping her gently but firmly. She closed her eyes in submission. The wave picked up speed dramatically like a powerful fairground rollercoaster until, like a woman giving birth, it ejected her onto the beach.

The warmth of the early morning sun on her face persuaded Annie to open her eyes. She found herself lying like a stranded crab with arms and legs splayed out on the wet sand. She blearily gazed up at the dawn's magic writing across the sky. Two white gulls circled above her limp body, squawking plaintively to each other. Unable to move, she lay there for some while, listening to the gentle lullaby of the ocean. The sea had rocked her, soothed her and had licked all her wounds.

Eventually, Annie raised herself to sitting, finding herself right beside the old pier. She realised she had ended her journey here, where it had all begun. When the quickening came it took her breath away... just for a second... and then it was gone; but she felt her body was glowing. She could feel the new life moving inside her... the special gift of motherhood.

As Annie struggled to climb the mountain of pebbles to the promenade, she gazed back for one last time before turning away from the cruel sea. A smile played upon her lips as her secret was confirmed now: a new beginning, a new life. How she hoped their baby would have Johnny's soft blue eyes.

Waiting for Susan

Deep within the night snow had fallen, serenely icing the meadows in a soft blanket of white and plunged the countryside into a blissful muffled silence; an ethereal world in suspended animation.

The next day, the dogs raced around exploring the transformed landscape and soon discovered that this cold, intangible substance was invigorating to roll in. As we skirted the lonely cemetery on our walk, the beech hedge whispered to us in the breeze, scattering tiny flakes of snow in a fine blizzard around me. All the graves lay hidden by the fall, apart from one in the far corner where the floral arrangements hadn't decayed but were frozen into still life structures. Draped with snow, all the lichen-covered obelisks loomed like bed heads for those sleeping there; a stark reminder of how temporary life is.

A small solitary figure, barely visible under a fountain of half-naked willow branches, stood by the church gate. She was about seven or eight with long fair hair cascading to her shoulders and fanning into a shimmering curtain, which cut across her green winter coat. One of the dogs charged towards her with hackles raised and broke into a bark. The girl's face, as waxen as a cream camellia, quickly fell into a worried grimace.

"Don't worry, she won't hurt you!" I shouted, quickly whistling Tabitha back to my side.

The child managed a weak smile, but her young face appeared sad and care worn. She looked anxiously behind her as though she was waiting for someone.

"Are you OK?" I asked.

"Yes… thank you," she said nervously, like a fragile moth caught out in the daylight.

I felt reluctant to leave her there alone, but the dogs

were impatient to reach open countryside. We scurried along beside ice laden streams, where clusters of primroses hid shyly along the banks. The dogs knew she was following us before I did. I glanced back and smiled at her; she nodded and drew her satchel nervously over her shoulder.

Eventually the girl set out along a parallel path to us, leading to Copse Farm. She walked quickly, occasionally breaking into a run but continually looking back to ensure we were in view. I was worried when she stumbled and dropped her satchel into a ditch; but then she waved and continued her journey. As the dogs bounced into the snowy meadow, I saw the child disappearing into a small cluster of farm cottages.

The panoramic views on the horizon caught my breath as we entered open fields bewitched into a wonderland of white. Naked trees held tight to shimmering buds, but young catkins danced on the breeze, shaking icy droplets down upon us. A plane zoomed like a rocket high above us, slowly ripping a white scar across the azure sky.

We walked until the greyness of the motorway split through the landscape, and then headed back past the farm where cattle munched on winter's fuel in pens. There were three little cottages in a line near Copse Farm, joined together by their front garden gates. I glanced up at the window of Rose Cottage and saw the little girl waving down at me. Her pale features creased into a grin as she held up a ragdoll, all floppy and pink.

The novice sun continued to sparkle in the sky and over the next few days our paths seem to cross as the girl in the green coat would be waiting under the willow, like a snowdrop. The dogs began to ignore her, so each day she'd walk behind us and then I'd watch her go safely along the path to the farm before she'd turn and wave at me.

One day, I was suddenly aware of her walking beside me.

"What are your dogs called?" she asked.

"Millie and Tabitha... Tabitha is the naughty one! What's your doll's name?"

"Susan," she said, focusing her grey eyes on mine. "I always take her with me wherever I go."

Our paths separated again, and she ran off waving.

A few days later, winter made another attempt to hold spring prisoner. Ice cold rain fell in a fine mist, creating a grey gossamer veil over the whole landscape. The fields were flooded, making our usual route muddy and too difficult to take. We pioneered the path like earthworms emerging from the depths. I turned up my collar against the March winds and trudged down the lane to Copse Farm, hoping I'd see the little girl at Rose Cottage. As I walked, head bowed against the wet, something pink caught my eye. I parted some grasses with my boot and there deep in the ditch lay Susan, all covered in mud. I stooped to snatch it before one of the dogs did and headed on towards Rose Cottage, squeezing water from the ragdoll as I went.

I hoped the little girl might be waving down at me from the window, but today the blinds were closed; in fact, all the curtains in the cottage were drawn shut. The dogs suddenly became subdued and went to sit either side of the front door, staring at me like sentinels. The sky had darkened suddenly, and rain began falling like a curtain; I was grateful to stand under the part-covered porch. I rang the bell several times and then resorted to loud knocking. Eventually a short, stout woman appeared at the side gate holding a red umbrella.

"They've gone away!" she shouted, looking me up and down suspiciously.

"Oh, I see," I said.

"They won't be back for several months; they've gone travelling around the world."

She seemed so unfriendly; I could only think she didn't like dogs.

"That's nice; but I think the little girl might be missing this," I said, holding up the bedraggled object. "I found it in a ditch."

Despite the reflection from the red umbrella, the colour drained from the woman's face and her mouth seemed to droop down at the corners. She stared at me hard and speechless. After a while the silence between us deafened me.

"Do you think you could keep it for when they come back?" I asked, gesturing for her to take it. "It might need a bit of a wash," I added.

"Oh no, I can't possibly do that," she muttered, turning her back as if to leave.

"Well, if you'd prefer I can take it home and wash it first?" I suggested.

The woman pivoted around, and I noticed pools of tears lying like half-moons in the lower rims of her grey eyes.

"No, I don't mean that. I mean I couldn't give it to them; I couldn't possibly distress them by bringing it all back to them... that's why they've gone away, to try and get over it."

I stared blankly at the woman but she seemed to be looking right through me.

"They need to get over the tragedy of it, you see," she said, quickly dismissing her tears with the back of a hand. "It's been several months now and they're still coming to terms with it... they're trying to help each other through it."

We seemed to be holding a conversation in two different languages. The weight of the water dragged my hair down over my forehead in the shape of little worms.

The rain on the woman's umbrella made a hollow noise like someone playing a tin drum and then the beats became a funeral march, melodically playing inside my head. I looked down at the doll and suddenly tears washed with the rain down my face.

"The little girl... she has died?" I asked.

The woman nodded like a stoic bulldog on the rear seat of a fast car. "She's buried back in the churchyard over there," she gestured into the distance.

Merry-go-round horses moved sedately around in my head whilst I tried to recall when I'd first seen the girl... it wasn't *months* ago, but barely a week. The icy rain slid down inside my raincoat like a serpent, slowly creeping along my arms and legs and down to my ankles. Like a deadly poison it turned my whole body cold and numb.

"Leukaemia it was," the women went on, her voice coming from somewhere far in the distance. "Emily was a beautiful little girl, like a delicate flower. Her parents took her to every doctor they could find. They just didn't give up... relentlessly searching for a cure. But it was no good; she was eventually taken from us. It nearly sent her mother crazy; they put her in a mental asylum for a time. It was so tragic... tragic... tragic," the voice echoed.

I stumbled as I felt the ground move beneath my feet.

"Are you alright dear?" the woman asked.

I could feel the heat from her red umbrella and the closeness of her pansy-like face pushed up near mine. "Do you want a glass of water or anything?" she asked.

"Did she miss the doll?" I stuttered, thinking that water was the last thing I needed.

"She cried for it for days when they took her to the hospice... Susan she called it. They looked everywhere but no one could find it."

I was aware of one of the dogs whining next to my boot.

Mechanically I clicked the leads on the dogs... I don't remember if I said goodbye to the woman; it all became a blur. I was still clutching Susan in my hand as I stumbled along the path. How could it be the same girl? If it was, how could I have seen her and walked beside her last week, when she had been dead for months?

I walked alone, holding the modest bunch of flowers. The whine of the metal gate broke the silence of the cemetery. I crept past ancient slabs of concrete where time had completely worn away any engraving... man's final attempt at immortality, failed. The newer stones were pristine and deeply cut with words from loved ones and special vases with holes in, some filled with flowers and others waiting to be remembered. I reverently approached the mound in the far corner where decaying flowers just held on to silhouettes of their previous glory. I had hoped to find a beautiful angel as a headstone, but there was just a simple little wooden cross. I carefully placed the floppy pink doll with the snowdrops there; and I knew that Emily would no longer need to wait for Susan.

Whiteout

He surfaced from yet another night in a sleepless trance, filled with visions of the stars falling from the heavens one-by-one and the night sky folding into complete blackness. Mark had been held captive in an ethereal void which drew all life around it into nothingness.

The bedroom curtains bulged in through the windows like giant lungs. Finally, the dawn was breaking, writing its message of hope across the sky. A small thread of courage developed in Mark as he quickly got dressed. Washing briskly, he deliberately chose to ignore the image in the mirror of a sepia stranger he no longer recognised. He made his way to the kitchen but felt no hunger; in fact, the very thought of food disgusted him.

After swigging back an energy drink, Mark summoned the elevator to take him down to his garage beneath the apartment block. He slid his wilting body into the car, then began setting his route.

"Your estimated time of arrival is 10.45 a.m.," confirmed the robotic voice.

Whilst the garage doors glided open, he sat back and closed his eyes, allowing the vehicle to hasten him away. Above the silent engine, there was a sudden groan from the pit of his stomach. He strained to fight the nausea sweeping over him.

"Activate manual controls," he shouted, grabbing the steering wheel from inside the dashboard cavity.

"Manual controls activated. Your arrival time is now indeterminate," a voice responded.

Brighton's coast road was deserted. Mark turned up the music and slammed his foot on the accelerator, embracing the adrenalin rush against the endless numbness. A light drizzle had started and the breeze was wafting pink blossoms across the road like confetti.

"I was going to marry her," he murmured beneath his breath as he pressed his foot down harder. She hadn't believed him; she'd laughed and told him he had no idea what love was.

That had changed the first time she took him to the cliffs above the Marina. On that day, just a week after his father died, Becky drove them out of the university campus towards the coast. Mark watched nonchalantly as the countryside unrolled in layers. They left her car at the cliffside car park and climbed the steep winding path to the summit. The wind rushed past them, playing drum symphonies in his ears. Walking up to the edge where the land disappeared into the distant horizon, he felt exhilarated. For a moment, it felt like he was flying.

"This is quite amazing! Where did you find this place?" he asked her.

"Oh, I used to come here with my friends from school... whenever we managed to escape."

"Now why would a nice girl like you want to escape from the prestigious St. Michaels?"

She paused. "You can inhale God here," she said, turning to face him, her silk blouse forming wings of gossamer in the wind. Her flaxen hair spiralled out from her head, transforming her into an angelic form of Medusa.

He gazed into her cornflower eyes, which he knew then that he would compare all summer skies to for the rest of his life. Inside he was dancing. He longed to kiss her but somehow his teeth got stuck to the sides of his mouth. Instead he stooped down and snatched a Marguerite daisy, placing it gently to her lips.

"That's lovely," she said, squeezing his hand. "I've got a flower press at home somewhere."

Simultaneously they glanced upwards, straining to see a lark fluttering and singing so high it was barely visible against the marbled sky.

"Oh, I nearly forgot... I've something else to show you," she smiled.

She led them to a door, overgrown with creepers and surrounded by long grasses and wild flowers.

"It was opened in 1910 as an air-raid shelter during the war. The school used it as a private access to the beach. It's a good place to hide when you're in trouble!"

"This is awesome," Mark said, rattling the gate.

"It's only opened on very special occasions, but if you know where to look..." she said, carefully edging her way alongside the concrete structure.

Becky disappeared, leaving Mark with the wind howling like a phantom through the gate. She reappeared slightly dishevelled with grasses poking out from her hair, grinning as she held up a rusty old iron key. At that moment, he knew for sure that he loved her.

She wriggled the key and he heaved aside the door. Gripping hands, they made their way along a dark tunnel, inhaling the escalating smell of the sea. Giggling like children, they headed towards a small dot of light and then, as if by magic, they appeared on the side of the cliff-face.

"Breath-taking," he sighed, grabbing hold of her hand.

It was a short walk down a narrow path to a vast empty beach. Laughing, they chased each other like mud skips until they were completely spent and too tired to go on. They lay down beside each other looking up at the seagulls; their plaintive cries told them stories of the vastness and cruelty of the ocean. They shared memories of their diverse childhoods, of their dreams and aspirations. As the sun slipped gradually beneath the horizon, they made love and spoke promises to each other that only they could ever know. Dusk settled in a grey cloak around them and, one by one, the stars ignited and rose into the velvet darkness.

Mark captured moonbeams in his hands and spread them over her closed eyes; she smiled contentedly.

They were reluctant to leave their special place, but Becky began shivering. He wrapped his jacket around her. She seemed to be glowing beside him in the tunnel until they emerged from the gate like fireflies, sparkling in the moonlight.

"You have reached your destination," the machine repeated.

Ford village was like any rural community these days: a few scattered houses, a derelict pub and a village shop which had been boarded up. Everything was delivered directly into people's homes now, thanks to EITS.

Mark's father had warned about the "Eyes-in-the-sky" from the early days. He'd seen it creep like a cancer into ordinary people's lives as entertainment, internet, telecommunications and much, much, more; until people became completely reliant on it. With their satellites, EITS monitored what people watched, what they wanted to eat or wear. It discovered everything that was important to them by carefully eavesdropping on conversations, listening through laptops and other devices until they could give people what they thought they needed, or wanted. Mark wondered if anyone else realised, or whether anybody really cared.

The warped wooden prison gates opened sluggishly. Ahead was an arched access where he needed stop at a barrier whilst a scanner swiped across his number plate.

"Good morning, Mr. McKenzie," said a friendly voice from the barrier machine. "Dr Scrivener is expecting you. Be so kind as to spread your right hand over the pad… OK, thank you. Now please remove it."

The barrier lifted, and a flashing green light ahead revealed his parking space. His car doors lifted like giant wings, allowing Mark to unfurl his frail body from the driver's seat.

"Good morning, Mr. McKenzie; so nice of you to come," said the ebony-suited man shaking Mark's hand briskly. "You're just in time to watch our first procedure of the day."

"Oh, great; thanks."

"I always appreciate interest from defence lawyers... as you will see, so many of your case failures end up here," Dr Scrivener grinned. "Follow me."

Scrivener was much taller than Mark remembered, and he moved swiftly for a man on the worst side of sixty. They reached a metal-clad door marked "Whiteout Unit".

"Why did you call it Whiteout?" Mark asked.

Scrivener's hand disappeared into a box and the doors ahead opened.

"Initially we called it "Wipe-out", but you can draw your own conclusions as to why that was changed," he snarled.

They headed through another set of doors and into a clinical area, resembling a huge plastic bubble. A body lay motionless on a table, clad completely in white. The doctor began washing his hands whilst a nurse tied a green apron around him. She tossed an apron over at Mark who was standing hesitantly by the door.

"The basis of this serum is a toxic protein which contains two pulsing isotopes," Scrivener said, thrusting his hands into latex gloves. "The first seeks out the aggressive regions in the brain to pacify them. The second attaches itself to the pituitary gland to eliminate sexual desire, making the patient impotent"

"That's clever. Is it painful?"

"Well, I'd like you to be the judge of that for yourself, Mr. McKenzie," Scrivener said.

The nurse reappeared holding a Petri dish. She smeared a pink liquid over the patient's left temple.

"Is the patient already anaesthetised?" Mark asked.

"Only a mild sedative has been administered."

Scrivener slowly unloaded a full syringe of fluid directly into the patient's temple, causing Mark to gag involuntarily. A vein immediately began to bulge and illuminate. As the liquid gradually travelled, other veins in the patient's head began to light up, eventually forming a blue pattern like a tattoo across the left side of the cranium.

"As you can observe, there is no discomfort during this procedure," Scrivener said, withdrawing the needle.

"That's it… simple!" he added, flicking off his surgical gloves. "Effective too; and the inmate will be up and about in approximately twenty minutes."

"What about all those lights buzzing around in the head?"

"They are merely electrical impulses which will die down shortly."

"Fascinating; but have any of these procedures ever gone wrong?"

"Occasionally there are small complications; for example, an inmate may be pregnant and the procedure will trigger a spontaneous miscarriage. Those cases are taken to theatre and the female is immediately sterilised."

"How can you be sure that Whiteout is reversible?" said Mark feebly, choking on his words.

"Don't worry, Mr. McKenzie," Scrivener smiled as he slapped Mark harshly on the back. "The isotopes can be retrieved with an antidote, injected in the same way. The solution attaches itself to the pulsing micro-silicones left by Whiteout and then passes them out of the body through natural wastage."

In a daze, Mark watched the nurse cleaning up whilst

Scrivener removed his protective clothing. The patient remained motionless. He thought of her... what they must have put her through. He struggled to compose himself.

"Does the blue tattoo effect remain across the head like that?"

"Not for long," Scrivener said, slicking his grey hair back through his fingers. "After a week or so, a silvery white scar begins to develop in those capillaries. Now... please do join me for some refreshments," he said, gesturing towards the exit.

A tray of coffee had been laid in a lounge area with glass all along one wall. Scrivener approached the one-way mirrors whilst eagerly downing his expresso. He beckoned to Mark.

"That group of inmates are going to the activity area prior to visiting the canteen for lunch," Scrivener pointed.

Mark watched them shuffling past, reminding him of cattle going to slaughter. Their eyes were blank to everything around them as they ambled along, focused only on staying in the line. Some of them nodded rhythmically whilst others were hampered by spasms which shook their bodies.

Mark's eyes were drawn to inmate 273. Her familiar frame was still slender and beautiful despite her shaved head; but there was something in her deportment that was clumsy. It scared him to see her like this.

"Can these patients still talk?"

"We don't refer to them as patients here, Mr. McKenzie... after all, they are criminals, and this is still a prison."

Mark controlled a sudden urge to swipe Scrivener around the head. As she turned, he saw the white pattern of scars on Becky's temple and something inside him shattered.

"Their intelligence has essentially been removed... they

96

are now functioning on a basic animal level," said Scrivener, directing his attention to a patient licking himself.

"Do they recognise people?"

"Unlikely I feel, as they barely make eye contact with each other," Scrivener said, sipping his second cup of coffee. "Which is why we have no need for wardens here. Governments love it; so much cheaper than previous penal systems."

Mark dragged his gaze from Becky; his heart was pounding fast. He wanted to take her now. He could smash the glass, jump down and grab her, killing everyone there, just to get her out of this godforsaken place. But that was not part of his plan.

"Just how many patients, I mean prisoners, have been given the antidote so far?" Mark asked, removing a notebook from his pocket.

"Well, thanks to the efficiency of prosecution lawyers, we have never needed to use it. As you would expect, the antidote is kept in a secret Government vault."

Scrivener put is cup down on the table thoughtfully.

"Would you like a tour of our young offender's unit?" he asked. "We reveal what the future could hold for these adolescents by involving them in the care of Whiteout inmates on a personal level. It scares the hell out of them!" he laughed. "What do you think, Mr. McKenzie?"

"At the risk of sounding rude," Mark replied, half-heartedly extracting his gaze from her, "would you mind if I take a brief walk outside first?"

The doctor looked puzzled, but Mark held up a hand-rolled cigarette. "I just can't manage to give up these little buggers."

"I presume you are on the smokers' register?"

"No chance of getting out of that one... EITS knows

everything about my bad habits," Mark smiled. "I'm proud to say my addiction is clearly recorded on my identity profile and I don't expect to receive any medical treatment when it finally finishes me off."

"Well that's very magnanimous of you, Mr. McKenzie," Scrivener scoffed. "Follow the corridor down to the garden, where hopefully you should go unnoticed."

Mark burst through the French windows, inhaling deeply. He walked across the compound area and levered himself over the fence into a field of wild grasses.

"The bloody bastards," he rasped, biting on the roll-up paper and shredding the tobacco through his teeth. He paced up and down angrily. "The evil fucking bastards… they have no right to take away people's souls!"

Above him dark clouds loomed like phantoms across the skyline; they hung so low he wanted to reach up and punch them. In the distance, a church spire sat like a dunce's hat in the corner.

"You can't keep God locked up in there, you pious bastards!" he shouted.

With a heavy heart, Mark reflected on the day he'd persuaded Becky to help him search for secret papers at Scrivener's house; he'd always suspected there was no antidote. She'd been reluctant to take the pistol, but he passionately pressed his lips on hers before leaving her outside the study to keep watch whilst he rummaged through drawers. Something must have disturbed the housekeeper and then all hell broke loose. The housekeeper's dog flew at Becky and unexpectedly the gun fired. He'd immediately wiped her finger prints off and instructed her to run; he didn't even have time to kiss her goodbye. He'd known that he was taking a chance that one of them wouldn't be coming back, but he didn't expect it to be her… the girl of happy endings, as he called her. Becky had been alone and, on the run, with police helicopters searching for a murderess.

Mark re-entered the Whiteout lounge, the nicotine still buzzing in his brain. "I thought you should know that I sent your papers to all the tabloids on my way here this morning."

"You mean the documents you stole from my home?" Scrivener retorted smugly.

"The public have a right to know that the antidote is completely useless; that is if it even exists at all!"

"The report merely stated that there was no point in using the antidote." Scrivener smirked.

"Exactly! Because you and I both know that the damage Whiteout does is completely irreversible."

Scrivener stood up.

"Did you really think I wouldn't piece together your connection with Rebecca Elliott?" he scowled. "It was only a matter of time before evidence was produced to bring you in. However, you seem to have saved us the trouble!"

Mark foraged in his pocket for the gun. "Take me to her," he demanded.

I'd be careful with that if I were you… according to your girlfriend, that thing has a habit of unexpectedly going off."

They barged into the canteen. Becky was hunched over her food tray. With tears in his eyes Mark bellowed her name. A cook appeared from the kitchen with a mouthful of food.

"What the hell?" he shrieked.

There was a sudden crack from the pistol and the cook staggered forward, landing heavily on a counter of dirty crockery. Smashing glass reverberated throughout the dining room. None of the inmates looked up.

"No going back now, Mr. McKenzie," Scrivener tormented

haughtily. "Give yourself up. Your girlfriend is one of the walking dead and you can gain nothing from all this."

"Shut up!" barked Mark.

With one arm he lifted Becky from the chair and cradled her. Her expressionless eyes, like a beautiful porcelain doll, sent a shiver darting down his spine; he felt more alone then, than he'd ever been in his life.

"YOU can come with us!" he demanded to Scrivener. "Or... I can get a canteen knife and cut your bloody hand off to open all the doors myself!"

They met no resistance on their way back to the car; the prison was as silent as a morgue.

"You must realise you are a condemned man," were Scrivener's last words as the car door lowered between them. The vehicle sped from the car park, breaking through the barrier and old wooden gates in its path.

She sat motionless beside him, her gaze focused on the hands folded in her lap.

"I love you, Becky," he said. "I came to rescue you... I did come in the end," his voice faltered. She was broken, and he knew he couldn't fix her; but only she could ever fix him. "I just want to be with you... nothing else matters," he whispered as he floored the accelerator.

The Cliffside car park was empty but for one or two cars. Mark grabbed Becky's hand and manoeuvred her into a clumsy embrace. His lips brushed hers momentarily.

"I failed you Becky, and I'm so sorry." He searched her dull, vacant eyes, hoping for some tiny response. "I did this to you, just as much as if I'd put the needle in your head... please forgive me?" Her body remained limp and static in his arms, mummified by the coarse prison cloth.

There were sirens in the distance. Mark tore his body from the vehicle and swept her out of the passenger door, leaving it abandoned like a broken eagle. She walked quietly beside him, all the way to the summit. Although it was daylight, the tunnel was dark and foreboding as they headed for the pinpoint of light at the end. As they emerged on the cliff face, the sun rolled out from a cloud suddenly, like a torch from heaven.

Mark turned to her. He could smell her fragrance beneath the harshness of the Carbolic soap. "It's time to say goodbye properly, Becks," he said, holding her shoulders square so that her hollow eyes aligned with his. "You have to come with me, so we can both be free."

As his foot slipped off the edge he pulled her into his arms and, just for a fleeting moment, her blue eyes illuminated in recognition. As they fell, words left her lips that he couldn't quite hear, but he thought she whispered his name before everything went black. It was so good to hear her voice again; for a moment, he felt like he was flying.

Mark stirred to the sound of metal instruments clanking beside him. Above him there was a white ceiling resembling a plastic bubble. He was completely paralysed. His body was infested with pain, but he recognised that he was high on morphine. A cold liquid was being smeared over his left temple.

"Good morning, Mr. McKenzie; it's so nice to have you back with us."

Lady in Red

An auburn flash streaked through the meadow. The red head paused and turned anxiously, her cat-like features distorted in fear; she realised she was far from the safety of her lover's den.

The hounds emerged through the swirling mist, screeching and snorting furiously, their legs hidden in the vapour. Close behind them she could hear the daunting calls of bugles and the rhythmic galloping of hooves over rough ground. The horses appeared legless and ethereal, shrouded in fog.

The hounds began to bay and the sight and the smell of her incensed them as they charged straight for her.

As she panted clouds, her russet body leapt over a fence into a hedgerow where her feet were punctured by a carpet of horned brambles. She sped on and courageously, plunging into an icy river which robbed her of her breath. She emerged bedraggled and wretched but still dashed on, twirling mist rising around her like steam.

She scrambled across a ditch, thick weed and dark mud clinging to her body. Nearby she could hear their feet splashing through water, chastising each other and barking angrily. She knew then that nothing could hide her evocative scent. She was tiring and they were relentless and closing in, hollering abuse as they stampeded after her.

All at once she realised there was nowhere to run; she was cornered and exhausted. Wide-eyed, she turned to confront her drooling and frenzied audience, their eyes glinting in desire as they shrieked at her. For a moment the birds became mute and all nature held its breath.

Amid the chaos of the kill, in some silent world, her life unfolded in visions before her as she died. She remembered her mother's sweet milk and the playful romps with her sisters in the sunshine.

She was tossed into the air and torn limb from limb; each dog greedily snatching her pelt from another, as they celebrated their victory. Although her body was ripped and abused, nothing could hurt Scarlett now.

Eventually they left her there; her limp body, crimson, torn and abandoned.

Alexander Road

The ocean changed its shape in a perpetual motion of dips and swells beneath a morning sky which boasted the clear blue everyone had longed for. The Southsea beach fronts were laden with families enjoying a typical British summer. Excited children grasped colourful buckets as they patiently watched their fathers hammering windbreaks into moist recently exposed sand. Clutching and snatching at shells, the tide had begun its retreat from the pebbles piled high against the promenade. All along this coastal stretch the new day was beginning, with a promise of ice creams, penny arcades and all the fun of the fair, amid the under-scents of chips and greasy sun lotion.

Gripping the lead securely, Elizabeth carefully navigated Bella to safely avoid streams of bicycles, joggers and the miniature blue train with enormous painted eyes. Bella was slow and sedate now and didn't cope well with stress. For a moment, Elizabeth paused to gaze out across the vast sparkling sea, far out to the distant horizon. The sepia shadows of several ships hung in limbo on the faded boundary between sky and ocean, motionless except to those who turned away for a time.

They crossed the road and vanished down a narrow street, leaving the chaotic seafront noises behind them. The grand beach front houses and hotels gradually disappeared. A few respectable B&Bs sprung up between shabby rented accommodation and flats where foxes had raided black bin liners abandoned in dishevelled front yards. Dust and debris collected on empty spirit bottles and discarded beer cans, amidst scatterings of dried dog faeces.

Along the cracked pavements, weeds grew high against crumbling brick walls covered in an eczema of lichen. Before she turned into Alexander Road, Elizabeth encountered an elderly drunk with several days of grey stubble on his sun-scorched chin. He gave her a toothless smile before reaching down to touch Bella's curly ivory coat. The man hovered there for a second or two, balancing precariously as if on a tightrope which he grappled to remain on, but never managed to control. As usual the retriever gazed up into his withered face, her kind brown eyes focusing on him whilst her whiskered jaw dropped open into a panting smile.

As they approached the black pointed railings of Alexander Park, Elizabeth could feel Bella's enthusiasm mount. They quickened their pace until they were engulfed in a peaceful green canopy of beech and oak. Taking their usual route from left to right of the big grass square, Bella was grateful to receive the freedom to roam off lead as she wished. Having completed the square three times, Elizabeth sat on a bench, allowing her arms to stretch across its width. She resisted frenzied tears hiding behind her dark green eyes, convincing herself that she was doing the right thing.

Bella returned to her owner's side and carefully settled herself down beside her feet. The gentle breeze ruffled the graceful fully-clad branches above them in a dance of their own. Debussy's *Clair de Lune* echoed in Elizabeth's mind, in tune with their motion. She allowed it to flow over her like the sound of the waves on the beach. They often sat there watching the world go by; Bella would twitch her nostrils and sniff the air periodically harnessing different scents. Their usual friendly Jackdaw would often hop along the path, searching for crumbs and blinking curiously at them.

A woman wearing impractical shoes walked her Westie quickly along towards them, gesticulating to her phone. The dog cautiously glanced over at Bella but was soon tugged along sharply like a little white puppet. As they left, it yapped briefly at the postman who'd propped his bike against the railings, juggling an armful of mail for residents in the square.

Soon an elderly couple entered the park, casually wandering hand in hand behind their bouncy Jack Russell. They eventually sat opposite Elizabeth; the man placing his hand gently on top of the woman's. They were too far away for her to hear their conversation or understand the topic of their smiles and laughter.

When the couple left, they nodded happily over at Elizabeth. Sudden unwelcome tears rose to sting her eyes. She sighed heavily, permitting them to roll and make damp tracks down her cheeks. They used to hold hands and gaze out into the world together like that... she'd questioned repeatedly why he had been taken from her. Only Bella had kept her going through those sad times.

A jogger appeared at the gate, her long lean legs pumping at the path. Elizabeth quickly swiped a tissue across her face and blew her nose, chastising herself for such stupidity. She said a prayer for him, as she always did, and inhaled a full lungful of air. Bella took this as a sign and rose slowly to her feet. She turned to focus those knowing brown eyes into Elizabeth's... they both knew... it was time to go.

The sun was beginning to weaken and fall as Elizabeth walked alone amid the cries and tantrums of exhausted children covered in salt, sand and remnants of ice cream, being coaxed and dragged back to cars by weary adults. She too must go back to the loneliness of her life, or at least find some way to carry on without the love of her life. So many long nights with pillows soaked by tears and a cold empty space beside her.

Elizabeth felt the restless pull of the ocean beneath her bare toes and the huge tug in her heart to go back to the veterinary practice, to scream and shout, shake Bella awake... and to return to Alexander Road.

The Soul Catcher

Spring sunshine washed the landscape clean and the gloom of winter was swiftly forgotten. Clusters of tiny primrose hid their faces shyly along the banks of newly flowing streams as new buds adorned every tree.

I wandered across a dew-covered meadow when an apparition caught my gaze across the sparkling pasture. The sight of it was so terrible, it made me tremble. As I approached the kneeling spectre, my face seemed like it was being caressed by blossoms, their fragrance sweeter than any I'd ever known.

Hearing my approach, the ethereal figure turned to me with eyes the size of saucers. It hovered in an unearthly way beside a corpse. Luminescent and almost invisible, the sun caught every angle of the face, like a mirror of many facets. Its hair consisted of rainbow coloured strands, constantly changing shape in tiny wafts of wind.

I dared to ask it who, or what, it was. The eerie being didn't respond immediately but gazed towards the sky.

"Sometimes they take a long while to come out; they are terrified of who I am. It is a lonely existence, but a task I do gladly," it sighed.

A strange sadness haunted the child-like features as it turned towards me with tears shining in its huge globes.

I knelt to touch the body on the ground. It was still warm with a blank stare which seemed focused on something very important in the distance.

"What are you waiting for?" I asked.

"The divine spark," it answered, holding forward a gossamer bag. "A child's soul sparkles so bright with all the pleasures of life; it lights up the world for a short time with a perfect crystal light. Their souls are so pure and bright, sometimes we take them early to light up the night sky," it said. "Others live to a very old age and they forget the joy of life; their souls become dull and hard. Their spark is so tiny it can barely be seen, yet it is still precious to the universe as it can spread light further into the darkness."

"What will you do with it... where will you take it?" I asked with lips a quiver.

The spirit smiled at me in such an innocent way causing a shiver to run through me. He gestured me to look closer.

I suddenly recognised the face... so many times just a shadow in the mirror. A veil of cool satin drew slowly across my face and a great sadness flowed over me in a colour... not black but a vacant grey. I lay down beside this strange being, made from some kind of bewitched glass.

"Is this all we are then," I asked, "just pieces of flesh and bone, born to die? Is this all life is, and if so, why?"

"You will soon understand," the being said, beckoning me towards the gossamer bag.

Blood Relative

An abrupt gust of wind rattled the metal bolts of the front door, its ancient faded wood gnarled with time and relentless storm beatings. A single candle danced precariously on the windowsill, erratic and alone, when it suddenly shivered and then died. Tabitha glanced up knowingly at Sarah and groaned, her gentle brown eyes drawn to the flames in the hearth fighting for life; she always sensed when 'they' were coming. Sarah hurriedly collected her coat and gave the dog a stay command.

"Just popping down to the Fox & Hounds, Mum," she called, as she poked her head fleetingly around the study door.

"But there's wine in the fridge, dear; please don't go out on a night like this!"

"It's not that bad, and I really fancy a bit of a stroll and a beer… we can have a glass together later."

As the front door slammed, Joan's forehead raised into a web of worry folds that she'd been carefully collecting for her daughter over the years.

Wind ripped through Sarah's clothing and spewed her thick auburn hair behind her into a long undulating funnel. Resignedly ascending the mountainous path to Alderley Edge, she gazed enviously through the pub window as she passed by. Bracing against the storm she looked down the cliffside at the autumn trees letting out arteries of bloody leaves into the bulging lakes beneath her. On the high ridge above her, evergreens stood poker straight seemingly unyielding to the gale. The sky began to darken as mighty festoons of cloud chased each other across the sky like sheep being herded into a pen. She began to shiver as the thick grey cloak of dusk wrapped its arms tightly around her.

Sarah always loved staying at the cottage by Lake Borrowdale as it held many happy memories for her; but she'd recently fled there in the knowledge that her aunt would be dead within a few days. Like the others, she knew that Aunt Phoebe would come to her soon; she'd come to haunt her and to occupy her psyche, invading all her innermost thoughts. It had always been this way as far back as she could remember. As Sarah's relatives lay dying, their souls would seek her out and she'd become their special place... their place of purgatory. By some quirk of fate, dead relatives managed to take up residence inside Sarah's head, sometimes staying for several weeks or even months at a time, manipulating her judgements and ruling her life. She'd once read somewhere that we're all made from recycled star particles and she wondered if her family's atoms were part of the dark matter holding the universe together, finding it difficult to escape from the earth. When they finally did go, she was left scarred and vacant.

It all began with her grandfather's death. She remembered her parents arguing on the three-hour journey to his house.

"We shouldn't be doing this Joan. She's got her first day at her new school tomorrow and she'll be exhausted," her father had said, his tall thin shape outlined by oncoming headlights.

"But it may be her last chance to see him, Edward; at least she'll have some memory of him."

Sarah knew little of Grandpa Harvey, apart from the dusty photos on the piano. He'd been injured in the war when a piece of shrapnel blinded one of his eyes. The old photos faded most of his features, but the prominence of his hooded eyes always jumped out of the picture and scared her.

As they drove up, they found an ambulance parked by

the front door with its rear doors open. The exterior of the house crawled with ivy and fat bodied spiders peering down at Sarah from a myriad of cobwebs. The old man had been a hermit for twenty years since his wife Violet left him and, as Sarah followed her parents over the threshold, she squeezed her nose as the putrefied odour of the house stung her nostrils.

"Now, you wait here whilst Mummy and I go upstairs," her father said as he lifted her on to a high kitchen stool. She anxiously scrutinized the dull and dishevelled room. "Don't worry, we'll be back soon," he added as he playfully messed up her chestnut curls.

Everything was still, apart from the beat of her heart inside her ears and the clock ticking away in the hallway. Above her there were muffled sounds of her parents' feet shuffling backwards and forwards across the bedroom floor. She lifted the lid on a rancid butter dish and screwed up her face as a cloud of tiny flies evacuated upwards in a spiral. Suddenly she heard whimpering noises through the ceiling and almost instantaneously there appeared a strange shadow lurking near the kitchen window. Something fuzzy swooped swiftly through the glass, heading straight towards her like a swarm of bees. An electric pulse surged through the side of her head, tingling down the back of her neck. She gasped as she began to fall slowly backwards from the stool. Like Alice tumbling down the rabbit hole, she tried to grab at something… anything, but the kitchen seemed to stretch out around her into a huge yawn. She heard the butter dish smash beside her as her chair cracked against the stone floor. Everything became dark.

"She could have a hairline fracture," a voice said in a dream.

Sarah's head ached, and her body seemed dull and lifeless. Voices seemed to fade in and fade out as she tried to catch tiny snippets of conversations. When she eventually woke up, she was in a small room with colourless walls. A splinter of light stole through a keyhole crack in the door. Her hair felt matted and sticky on the pillow beneath her. She was alarmed by the feeling that something was watching her from a hidden place, somewhere deep inside her; it lingered in the darkness, secretive and quiet.

"Mum!" she cried out.

Her mother rushed in. "It's alright darling," she said, switching on the light.

"I don't like it here… I want to go home."

"Of course dear, but the doctor wants to make sure you're OK before we can make our way back home."

Sarah again felt the strange presence hiding close to her and struggled to sit up. She panicked and cried out bringing her father and the doctor rushing into the room.

"Carry me Daddy," she said, reaching her arms out to him.

The doctor shone a light into her eyes and asked her questions about how she felt. "I think a regular dose of paracetamol will keep the headache away," the doctor said. "But I think your daughter will be fine."

"There Joan… she's fine!" her father said with half a grin. "Let's get this girlie home; we can't do anything more here."

Her parents were silent on the car journey home. The rhythmic drone of the engine and the oncoming headlights illuminating the interior of the car comforted her. She didn't know what it was, but she was sure something was there in the back of the car with her.

"You are going to have an extra holiday before starting your new school," said her father as he carried her up to her bedroom.

"Yes, and we are going to buy you a special new dress

112

for the funeral," said her mother, pulling back her duvet. Sarah could tell she had been crying.

Life appeared to return to normal for a few days, but unbeknown to her parents, Sarah's world had become dark and unreal. The unknown presence lingered close to her at all times... she was never alone.

The funeral day arrived. Sarah put on her new black velvet dress and sneaked into the dining room where the highly polished coffin stretched serenely across the room, rigid and still. The icy atmosphere caught her breath as if it might snap like a biscuit. She peeked over the casket edge, noting the shimmer of red satin against her grandfather's dull porcelain skin; the alabaster cadaver was shrouded like a rose within folds of ruby silk. Her grandfather didn't seem as scary with his eyes closed. But a voice nearby whispered to her, instructing her as to what she must do.

Her mother appeared with a tear stained face. She silenced Sarah with her forefinger. "Don't worry, darling, I should have explained that when we die we go straight into the light of heaven." But little Sarah was desperate to tell her that not all of them do.

Sarah then made her way through the house in search of Violet's new husband, Peter. An intangible feeling of hate bit at her heart. She snatched the knife from the cheese platter and stormed towards him... blood surging angrily through her frail network of veins. His eyes grew wide with terror as she approached him, and his mouth dropped open as he spotted the knife. With one eye closed, Sarah plunged the knife deep into Peter's chest. Flesh peeled away from the blade as she withdrew it and her naked forearms turned as scarlet as her new shoes. The room seemed to hold its breath.

Then pandemonium erupted. Cries and shrieks only echoed her own distress, but no one listened to her cries.

She sat on the floor, isolated and scorned, in an area full of chaos. The dark spirit inside her gave a huge sigh of satisfaction.

"It was uncanny," Violet bleated to the policeman, tears streaming down her face. "Her little face had the same grimace as her dead grandfather!"

Not long after, Sarah and her parents left with the policeman; nobody spoke a word to her. The police car drew up at a huge ancient building where ugly stone faces peered down at them from the battlements.

Where are we going, Mummy?" she asked.

No answer came. She reached for her mother's hand as they entered the building; it was trembling.

"Is this a hospital?" she asked as their footsteps echoed down the draughty corridor. "They don't look very sick," she observed, as she peered into half lit bedrooms.

They reached a small, dimly lit room. A nurse with a pale face and white uniform stood up as they entered. She silently lifted Sarah on to the bed and started to unbuckle her shoes.

"We have to go now, darling," her mother said. Her voice sounded funny and she kept looking at the floor.

"You'll be safe here," explained her father.

"Don't go!" Sarah shouted.

The nurse's eyes were cold and emotionless as she pinned Sarah's body to the bed.

"This won't hurt," she said.

The needle stung briefly in her leg and then all images around her wilted into strange exotic flowers.

As she became semi-conscious, she felt as though she was locked in a small dark tomb. People came in and out of the room many times, but she was incapable of speech. Time had no essence. The stinging needles were a regular occurrence, but she knew no day or night. She was suspended in a

114

chrysalis-like existence which seemed endless. At some point during this nightmare, she was aware of a strange trail of dark dust entering her head; it swirled around, searching like a hungry flock of gulls. Her body trembled as it attached itself to the dark presence inside her and, with a brittle screeching noise, the dark spirit entwined within the dust was dragged from her.

Sarah gasped and woke suddenly, unable to move as she was wrapped up like the baby Jesus had been in her school nativity play. Her terrified eyes moved jerkily around the room, noticing beams of light highlighting dust particles sparkling in the air; but the dark dust and the presence had gone. At that moment a nurse came in with a bowl and sat beside her.

"You must eat," she said, pushing a spoon through the dry and cracked folds of Sarah's lips. She gagged, but the nurse persisted in getting the mixture down her throat.

After a day or two they untied Sarah from the white linen web and she was permitted to feed herself with a little plastic spoon. The stern-faced nurse left two books at her bedside; one of them was Hans Christian Anderson's Fairytales with colourful picture templates. She read it from cover to cover, over and over again. There was a tiny window in the door of her room where eyes occasionally flickered, then disappeared. She always heard the key turn in the lock outside after the nurses left, but that didn't bother her as she felt free… the dark presence of her grandfather had finally left her.

"Are you ready to answer some questions?" the doctor asked as he sat at the end of her bed. He reminded Sarah of a large eagle, with sharp blue eyes and a beak of a nose.

"I want to go home," she said.

"And you can… soon. We want to help you, Sarah," he said.

His questions were strange, but she tried to answer them

as best she could. The doctor listened carefully, scribbling down some notes in a file with her name on it.

"I didn't like it when it made me do those things," she told him.

"So," he sighed. "Do you believe it was the spirit of your dead grandfather?"

Sarah nodded.

"And you think that this spirit has now gone away?"

"Yes I do. But please can you stop it coming back?" she asked.

"Of course," he said as he got up to leave.

She waited patiently in the dim echoing corridor whilst her parents spoke with the doctor in frightened whispers in his office.

"Schizophrenia?" The strange word wafted under the door like a nasty odour.

Sarah was taken home and was to be home-schooled for the time being. However, despite taking all the tablets the doctor gave her, Great Aunt Clara's spirit arrived one day in a sudden flurry. At the age of nine, Sarah's head felt like the monkey house at the zoo. She tried to hide in a small corner of her mind whilst Clara's thoughts, memories and desires bounced around her head. Before too long, the mischievous presence of Clara had complete control of everything Sarah did.

"What's that book you're reading dear?" her mother asked before snatching the copy of *Lady Chatterley's Lover* from her daughter's grasp.

Sarah began to suffer with a recurring nightmare where a small child is floundering in the middle of a huge lake. In her dream Sarah drops down into the icy water, feeling it pressing heavily on her chest. She calls out to the child as she tries to swim out, but waves start to push her back to the shore and soon her body is trapped against the bank. The water rises higher and higher up to her throat and over her mouth, but she is paralysed; then she would wake.

Clara had always hated Sarah's mother, Joan, making Sarah say vicious and nasty things to hurt her; things that Sarah never meant. She began stealing from her mother's purse, the local shop too, and smoking cigarettes in her bedroom. Eventually her parents took her to a different type of hospital, where children were "reformed", they told her. Sarah hated it there.

"They give me disgusting medicine all the time and at night people scream and shout all night," Sarah told her mother. "When can I come home?"

"Soon," she answered, stroking her hair. "When you are better, dear."

Every night in her restless sleep she was dragged to the bottom of the ocean, where she sat bewildered and tormented by voices telling her that she was useless and no good.

Then, for some reason unknown to Sarah, she woke up on the morning of her tenth birthday and Clara had gone. It must have happened whilst she was sleeping she thought; it was the best birthday present she could ever wish for.

Over the next few years Joan continued to home-school her daughter and they became very close. Arguments developed between her parents making Sarah hide away in her bedroom, listening to their raised voices; she felt responsible. She spent many hours examining her face in the mirror… it was ethereal… she had no idea who she was.

In the summer of that year Sarah was sent to a farm in Hampshire to stay with her Uncle Ernie, his wife Marjorie and their daughter Linda who was two years older and Sarah's only cousin. Linda was heavy set with a tanned skin, and a long length of silky ebony hair. Marjorie's family had originated in Ireland and were Romany gypsies.

"There's nothing wrong with you!" Marjorie said, looking Sarah up and down. "So, you won't be getting out of any chores while you're here." She handed her a bucket of grain. "Go feed the chickens now; otherwise there'll be no supper."

She'd never seen chickens up close, at least not with feathers on. She sprinkled some grain for them and stood watching as their beady eyes spotted the food. Two of them strutted suspiciously towards it, carefully lifting one crimson claw then putting it down and allowing their jerkily heads to catch up. Suddenly Linda grabbed her waist and lifted her into the air, bucket and all. She swung her round and all the grain cascaded about them in a circle.

"You're here at last!" she cried. "I've been so excited... you're going to sleep in my room, and we're going to tell each other stories all night."

Linda lived in a world of fantasy, in which Sarah was only too pleased to take refuge. She soon found out that, although Linda was older, her reading skills were poor; but her imagination was full of stories about vagabonds and pirates, highway men and damsels in distress. Most evenings she implored Sarah to read her *Kidnapped*. Sarah confided in her about the spirits who sometimes came to live in her head, but Linda just laughed and told her to "Just kick 'em out!" One night whilst Sarah was shivering in a nightmare, Linda crept out to the shed and brought in two of the four-week-old brown puppies. They slept in between them all night and from then on Sarah slept nightmare free for the whole summer.

Apart from chores, the girls spent their days exploring the overgrown orchard and riding ponies up and down the field bareback, pretending to be on a ranch. When the sun began to set they'd climb trees to watch birds swarm in like clouds against the pink sky. Linda pretended she knew how to speak their language and Sarah laughed at her funny bird calls until her sides ached. They'd snuggle up to the puppies each night, making a den for them all under the covers with torches, treats and snacks.

At the end of the long summer, Sarah's parents came to collect her. They seemed so much happier together now and were holding hands. Sarah was pleased but very sad to be going home.

"There ain't nothing wrong with this 'ere girl," Marjorie told Sarah's parents.

"Except, she talk's funny!" added Linda, laughing and hugging Sarah around her neck until her eyes bulged.

Linda began to cry as Sarah's bags were loaded into the car. The car was pulling slowly away when Linda knocked rapidly on the window, running to keep up. Sarah opened the window and Linda carefully placed one of the brown puppies on to her lap.

"She'll keep those nightmares away," Linda whispered. Both girls waved until they were out of sight.

Sarah called the puppy Tabitha and life became calm and peaceful from then on. Her parents allowed Tabitha to sleep in her bed every night.

About a year later, Sarah woke with a strange feeling of sadness. She looked at the tiny scar on her palm which she had forged with Linda as blood sisters. In her mind's eye she saw an image of Linda laughing as she slipped off her pony and shouted, "Oh no, I've peed myself!"

Linda never spoke about the hospitals she'd been in or the suffering she'd endured... no one had ever mentioned the word 'remission'. Sarah thought she heard Linda's voice echoing in her head, "Mum's right, there's nothing wrong with you!"

Later that morning Joan told Sarah that Linda had been

ill for many years with leukaemia and had died the previous night. Linda could never know how, in her short lifetime, she had lit up the world for Sarah. Sarah knew she'd gone directly to somewhere light and bright, somewhere where pirates play, and ladies dance all day... and all night. She wasn't in need of Purgatory.

Grandma Violet died next. She seemed to want to make up for any wrongdoing from her past so Sarah found herself in church most days and three times on a Sunday – the vicar began to look quite perplexed when he spotted her sitting at the back of the church again. With blunt scissors, she hacked her hair short to use it as a nest for an abandoned baby bird. She cycled around the village feeding neighbours' pets and volunteering to clean elderly ladies' houses.

On one of her infrequent visits to Sarah's mother, Aunt Phoebe had asked if her niece could join them for tea.

"What have you done to her, Joan?" Phoebe said, throwing her hands up in despair. "A girl of her age should be wearing make-up and dating boys!"

"Well we can't all be the same as you, Phoebe," her mother said.

"There's nothing wrong with being different, but Sarah looks like Joan of Arc!"

This worried Sarah as she'd read somewhere that Saint Joan had been burnt at the stake for hearing voices. Sarah decided she really disliked her Aunt Phoebe.

The day Violet left, Sarah was able to tell her mother things that only she and Violet could have known about their relationship. Gradually Joan began to believe that her daughter had been telling the truth all these years; she spent hours looking back at their family tree. But in the meantime, Sarah's father decided it was time for him to leave. Sarah stood at the top of the stairs, listening to her parents talk in the hallway.

"As much as I love Sarah," she heard her father say. "Let's face it, Joan, she's ruined our marriage. Before too long she will strike and kill someone again... she should be put away for her own and everyone else's good."

"But she is dealing with it, Edward... there is much more to all this than you think. She wouldn't hurt us and she is getting better as every day passes."

"Well, if you believe that, it's you that needs your head examined," he snapped as he dragged his suitcase towards the door. "Come to think of it, perhaps that's where she gets it from; your family have always been weird!"

Sarah slept in her mother's room for several months after that. She often listened to her mother tossing and turning throughout the night, speaking in a strange dream language.

As the storm whipped and punished Sarah, she knew it was time for Aunt Phoebe to arrive. She'd had five failed marriages and it was rumoured she had poisoned two of her husbands. She'd had so much plastic surgery that the corners of her mouth resembled a military moustache. Sarah always felt uncomfortable in her presence... unworthy of living, somehow. How could she ever survive possession by Aunt Phoebe's spirit? It always took so long to regain her life once 'they' had gone, and she was left damaged by their many traits and influences.

About a year ago Sarah had met James, a fellow psychology student. In recent months they'd become close and spent the long summer holidays in each other's company. She couldn't bring herself to tell him the whole truth about her past but only that she'd suffered from depression. He was a good listener and never judged; he called her his guinea-pig patient... his work-experience. He believed that characteristics were derived from inherited genes and yet it was possible to by-pass them. He thought the child Sarah tries to rescue in her dream was herself. Phoebe would come and seek her out soon, and then her relationship with James wouldn't stand a chance.

Sarah's legs began to ache with the exertion of the steep climb. When she reached the summit with the wind roaring past her ears like a lion, the landscape below appeared to have been carefully manicured by some supreme gardener. Beneath the poker bracken, tiny houses peered shyly over the hedgerows, their windows beginning to glow with evening candles and firelight. She carefully peered over the edge… it was a long way down, much further than she'd anticipated. The craggy cliffside opened below like a gaping mouth. She'd always been afraid of heights, but strangely tonight she felt no fear. She imagined the news report: 'Unbalanced twenty-five-year-old psychology student falls from rocky crag whilst walking.'

The lake below looked just like her dream and for a moment she thought she glimpsed a shape floundering in the centre. An army of grey cloud obscured the last of the autumn sun as it slipped rapidly from the sky. But then a vibrant ribbon of turquoise appeared and a thought occurred to her… above all the clouds, the sky was always blue. A sudden glimmer of hope grew inside her. She realised that whatever dark and terrible thing had led her to this place was something much older, murkier and more terrifying than any of her relatives had been. She could feel its grip on her as her body teetered on the edge of the precipice. With all the strength she could muster, she dragged herself away. Trembling she turned and headed back the way she came.

She began to jog, and an unexpected strength pulsed through her veins. She told herself she could survive Phoebe, just like she had all the others; she was better equipped to deal with those demons now. She wasn't mad like all the doctors thought. She could make a new start when it was all over and at least her mother would have a daughter and at least she wouldn't let her down. A voice called out in the wind... *was it Phoebe?* she wondered. She heard a bark in the distance and saw her mother climbing the rocky path with Tabitha hobbling along beside her.

"Thank God you're alright," she shouted above the storm. "I came to tell you that Phoebe was adopted!"

"What?"

"Phoebe was adopted!" Joan repeated as she approached her daughter. "Nobody knew... our parents kept it secret, even from her."

"Oh, Mum..." she said, lurching into her waiting arms. They were both shaking and Sarah began laughing, with tears washing down her face.

"Well, I did have some suspicions," Joan said, trying to calm her breathing after the exertion of the climb. "It wasn't just the lack of family resemblance, but something just wasn't right."

Stumbling over rocks in the dark, they made it back to the Fox & Hounds. Sarah handed her mother a large brandy and slugged another back herself before sitting beside her. They both stared blankly into space, as the bar began to fill with people and noise.

"How did you know where to find me?"

"Your phone rang, and a very nice lad called James asked me who I was. He felt sure something was wrong... something about a dream you both talked about. He told me to look for you near a lake."

"He does care," whispered Sarah.

"Tabitha led me right up the path to where you were," Joan said, tipping the glass to taste the last drop.

Sarah felt a tail wagging against her leg under the table

at the mention of her name. She thought of Linda and smiled, remembering her laughter and their puppies.

"What were you doing up there alone, dear?"

"Nothing really. I just needed to go there... so I could come back."

Prologue – Sarah had waited and hoped her mother would come to her after she died. But she'd once told her daughter that she would head straight for the light and all she'd leave behind were their memories.

The Tinder-Box

Buried deep within the vaults of Bridlesmere church lies a box… a small box, approximately ten inches square… just big enough to fit a man's face in.

On a brisk and sunny September morning, children dragged their feet reluctantly back to school in their new shoes and an eerie silence fell over the playgrounds of Bridlesmere village. Later that day an explosion ripped through the 12th century parish church of St. Mary.

Phones rang relentlessly at Chungford police station. Daniel Jonah fidgeted in his worn leather chair, aggravated by each ring tone being slightly off time with another.

"Where the hell is Brenda?" he roared, charging over to the nearest handset, his tweed jacket flapping around him like bellows. "Chungford Police," he snapped. The caller hung up.

He suddenly remembered that Brenda had left early for a doctor's appointment and that the area switchboard wouldn't take over for another hour. He grabbed another handset and spoke more restrainedly.

"Is that you sir?" the voice said.

"Charlie… where the hell *are* you? The phones are going mad here!… What do you mean Bridlesmere church has been bombed?"

"Well, not exactly bombed… I suppose you could say it was an act of God."

"God in a church… well there's a novel one," Jonah mumbled beneath his breath.

"Early findings suggest a lightning bolt," Charlie continued.

"Hmm," he said, glancing at his watch. "Tape off the building and we'll get stuck in first thing tomorrow."

"Trouble is, sir, we have a corpse at the scene… turns out to be the vicar."

"Oh… alright," Jonah said with a sigh. "I'll call Pathology and drive on over."

Meanwhile – somewhere in Tibet

Longchenpa slowly detached himself from the sphere of light. He'd just witnessed another life lost in the pursuit of truth. He felt spiritually drained, but his scrawny half-naked body remained poised on the square plinth. From high in the green Himalayan Mountains he could see all the struggles of mankind through his box of light.

The sun began to lower in the sky and he anticipated the gift of nourishment. A young monk entered the temple carrying a small tray. His movements felt like a gentle breeze and Longchenpa inhaled the aroma of jasmine flowers. He could sense the sweat on the monk's brow, hear the dust falling from his feet and feel the energy of the outside world. The Samanera bowed and scraped his chin along the floor beneath the Lama as he crawled backwards from the sanctuary.

Longchenpa sighed as he sunk into his renewed isolation. He'd lived 100 years this way but now saw a time when he could find complete enlightenment. Many had searched for it, but he knew the box would come to him soon and he waited patiently, longing for that illuminating void.

Jonah gazed into the Victorian terraced houses along Church Lane, their windows peeping shyly over well-groomed privet hedges. Suddenly a black Mercedes confronted him in the middle of the road. Jonah swerved into the ditch, foul-mouthing from the window as the car disappeared down the lane behind him. Fingering his cigarette packet, he waited for his blood pressure to fall; his pigeon coloured moustache twitching agitatedly.

He drove on into a converted barn complex, admiring the impeccably manicured gardens with an Ornamental Well and Dovecote. Nearby stood St. Mary's, a simple Saxon church which was recorded in the Doomsday Book. As he entered the graveyard, Jonah noticed that a strange stillness filled the churchyard and he recognised an unusual odour. Seagulls hung like kites in a bright innocent sky, with no sign of a storm. Approaching the shattered east window, he tiptoed over coloured glass pebbles scattered about like boiled sweets. The remaining pieces of stained glass were huddled behind the window cages like frightened birds.

Tossing nicotine gum into his mouth, Jonah walked towards the entrance. The black wooden door was dwarfed by an enormous hollow yew which cast long shadows over the church, its mighty branches hovering over some unusual graves mounded with lichen-covered red bricks. Folding his lofty frame under the door arch, Jonah found the forensics team already at work, whilst the ambulance crew waited patiently beside the corpse. Standing amongst the debris, he pondered on how lightning could obliterate such sizeable ancient flagstones. The vicar's body lay crumpled in the foetal position beside a cavernous hole, his face hidden within folded arms and his purple robe splayed behind him like a superhero.

"Who's the elderly lady in the corner?" Jonah whispered to Charlie.

"Maureen Baker, the verger; she lives nearby and came running when she heard the explosion. The church door was locked, but she was first to discover the body."

"I'll chat with her whilst you go and interview any witnesses at Saxon Meadow; it may be a retirement haven, but surely they can't *all* be bloody deaf."

"Hello, Maureen… Detective Inspector Daniel Jonah," he said, taking hold of her hand. "Are you OK?"

The woman's speckled hand shook, and tears welled in her eyes. "*I'm* alright, but what about the Father's family?"

She wore her hair swept back into a comb and Jonah could see she'd once been a beautiful woman. Jonah perched on the pew beside her.

"Why do you think Father Brian locked himself in?"

"I don't know," she said thoughtfully. "I can only think he must have been deep in prayer, or perhaps writing his next sermon."

Maureen accepted Jonah's offer of a lift home. A soft rain splattered the window screen as the car pulled away.

"Can you tell me a little bit about Father Brian, Maureen? What sort of man was he?"

"In my eighty years, I've never known a better family man; he attracted so many young people to our little church. But some parishioners didn't like his style."

"Do you think he had enemies in the village then?"

She paused thoughtfully. "I think the Diocese felt he went against many of their rules."

The heavens opened as Jonah watched Maureen dash nimbly into Jasmine Cottage. As he drove back to Chungford, Jonah continued to speculate as to why the body wasn't torn apart like the flagstones were.

When he arrived home Jonah's dog came bounding to greet him. He opened the back door, flicked the kettle on and left a voicemail for Charlie to meet him at the morgue in the morning. The Labrador stood by the apple tree with one leg extended for many minutes. Mounding dog food into the dish, Jonah promised himself he'd take Leo along tomorrow.

Jonah had known Jeff, the Coroner, for many years.

"What've you bought me this time, Dan?" he asked, withdrawing the cadaver from the cold-locker.

Sunlight pierced the morgue windows, highlighting the vicar's auburn hair; Charlie gasped at the rapid disintegration of his face.

Jeff bent over the body like a crane. "Unusual breakdown of facial tissue."

Jonah heard Leo quietly breaking wind beneath their feet and stifled a grin.

"It's very curious… nothing like I've seen before," Jeff said, twitching his handlebar moustache and glancing under the slab. "Does the dog really need to be here, Daniel?"

"Oh yes; Leo's a real sniffer dog, Jeff."

Charlie covered her mouth with her hand.

"The abnormal cell degeneration may have been triggered by the explosion; more likely though, this man was probably already ill and dying. I'll arrange for a post-mortem immediately."

Jonah was relieved to embrace fresh air again. "How did it go at Saxon Meadow, Charlie?"

"Mrs. Burrows heard the explosion whilst cleaning her windows and I'm going back now to take her statement."

"Good; and I'll pay the widow a visit."

Despite ample boot space, Leo decided to climb into the passenger seat. Jonah allowed some much-needed air into the car as he drove to Bridlesmere.

Built in flint with a grey slate roof, the Vicarage had Georgian sash windows framed by a prolific rambling rose. Jonah tied Leo to a tree and crunched down the gravel path, a straggly holly hedge pricking at his legs. A middle-aged woman peered around the door at him.

"Mrs. McCormack?… DI Daniel Jonah; do you mind if I come in?"

"If you must," she croaked. The woman moved quietly like a shadow through the dimly lit hallway and led them into an austere study. She turned suddenly, a dark curtain of hair swaying across her grey, haunted features.

"They killed him you know!" She clenched her jaw as tears snaked tiny pathways down her ashen skin.

"*They?*" he asked; his attention drawn to a portrait of the family.

"The Episcopal polity," she answered, fixing her hollow eyes on him. "Brian sought the truth and began delving into things. The Archdiocese demanded he stop... but he wouldn't; so, they got rid of him!"

As three small girls appeared at the doorway the woman broke into sobs; they ran in and smothered her. Jonah felt unexpectedly emotional, deciding it was time for him to withdraw. He briefly studied the family portrait again before finding his own way out.

Jenny sat on her usual bench in the Bishop's Gardens with a book in one hand and a sandwich in the other. Her name appeared like a sigh on Jonah's lips. The sunlight danced through her chestnut hair which was scooped upwards to reveal her long elegant neck. They used to sit side by side on that bench with heads huddled together as she read out bits from her favourite crime novel.

Before Jonah could stop him, Leo bounded over excitedly. Watching from a safe distance as the pair fussed over each other, Jonah suddenly caught Jenny's glare and decided to make his way over.

"Do you mind if we join you?"

"Be my guest," she replied coolly, her face softening as Leo sprawled across her lap.

"Another crime novel I see," he said bravely. An awkward silence fell. "How are you keeping, Jenny?"

"Why would *you* care, Daniel?" she said, gazing up at him with Hazel eyes he just wanted to fall into.

"Silly question," he said. He couldn't blame her for hating him; he consoled himself that hatred was at least better than indifference.

"You should know that I've found someone else."

Jonah coughed, as a subtle knife slid beneath his ribcage.

Her face crumpled into a frown. "You didn't care about my feelings when you were with *her*."

"It wasn't like that, Jenny."

"What was it like then?"

Jonah stood awkward and silent.

"You still work with that Charlotte, don't you?"

"Charlie was a mistake, Jenny… it didn't mean anything."

"Well, it meant something to me!" A single tear passed delicately down Jenny's left cheek. "What do you want anyway?"

"Some advice about a case."

"Class starts in five minutes," she said, looking at the dainty watch he'd bought her.

"Can you explain what the Episcopal polity is about?"

"Are you joking? Your own grandfather was a vicar!"

"I told you, Jenny, he was a harsh man who I barely knew; if anyone could put a lad off God, it was him!" He whistled for Leo. "For what it's worth, Jenny, it was the biggest mistake of my life."

"You could come back after class; I'll help you for old times' sake," Jenny whispered.

Jonah's heart leapt into his mouth.

"Let's say five thirty; and you can buy the coffee," she said.

Back at the station, Jonah was finding it difficult to contain his elation at meeting with Jenny. Charlie entered the office.

131

"What happened with the old folk at Saxon Meadow, Charlie?"

"Well, it appears most of them *are* actually deaf!" She giggled. "Mrs. Burrows remembered a clap of thunder and saw several flashes of lightning. But the interesting thing is," she said, sliding like a cat onto the end of Jonah's desk, "she reckons the thunder clap came 20 minutes or so *before* the lightning."

Trying to avoid eye contact and remain composed, Jonah began searching his pockets for gum.

"The gardener heard an explosion, and he confirmed the same timing," Charlie continued. "Apparently the light was so powerful it pierced through the tiles of the spire and lit up the weather vane!"

"Is there any news from forensics yet?"

"Not the full report, but they've found traces of Nitrosamine," she said.

"RDX? That would explain the white crystals near the crater and that smell. I think Father Brian was an Army Chaplin at some point in his life; but why would he blow up his own church? Find out if there were any tombs or catechisms beneath the floor, Charlie; If necessary go back to the 12th century."

Charlie smirked and nodded.

Jonah picked up his jacket. "In the meantime, I'm going to the Registry Office before it closes."

"Planning a wedding, sir?"

"No… I believe that Father Brian may have had a son; a boy with bright auburn hair."

At the café, Jonah tied Leo to a drain pipe whilst Jenny found a quiet table in the corner. He discreetly related the mysterious circumstances surrounding Father Brian's death. She answered all his questions; then he struggled to think of more, just to keep her there. How Jonah adored all those familiar laughter lines... he could map out everyone in his sleep.

"So, what you're saying is that the Bishop controls and dictates everything that goes on in churches within his Diocese."

"Yes, within reason," Jenny said, finishing the last dregs of her hot chocolate. "Sometimes there's a council meeting called a Synod and they make decisions about the policies of the Diocese, but the Archdiocese can always overrule any of them."

"Does the Synod meet here in Chungford?"

"Yes, in a special upper room in the cathedral. Chairs are sited around the square of the room and each one is engraved with the name of a deceased Bishop. No minutes are kept."

"So basically, the meetings are secret then?"

She nodded.

"Do you think we might meet up again, Jenny?"

"I'll have to talk to Matthew about that. He's a very sensitive person... a talented musician and poet."

"Ah, you deserve someone cultured after having a rough and ready, like me."

They shook hands awkwardly at the café door before going their separate ways. Jonah felt suddenly consumed by emptiness. The dog led him home.

The next morning Jonah drove to St. Mary's. He was surprised to find it invaded by vehicles. There were several white vans marked with the name of a local stonemason and a familiar black Mercedes perched awkwardly on the grass by the gate.

Jonah left Leo draped across the front car seats. Inside, the church was brightly lit with powerful lamps aiming into the crater. There were lowered voices beneath the floor and sounds of rock being broken up. A man in a black suit appeared at the top of a ladder.

"As you can see, we're making a start on repairs to the masonry," he said, grooming dust off his shoulders.

"I'd have thought it was a bit premature for that," Jonah said, peering into the fissure.

"Forensics gave us the go ahead," the man replied flatly.

Aware that the man had left, Jonah rushed from the church in time to see the Mercedes drive off at speed. For a moment he was tempted to follow but decided to make a visit to Jasmine Cottage instead.

"Who is it?" Maureen called, looking inquisitively into Jonah's face.

"It's Detective Jonah… remember from yesterday?"

"Of course, Daniel, do come in."

Jonah followed Maureen into the house, noticing how she caressed the walls as she walked; she seemed so much more frail and unsteady than yesterday. She led them into a small parlour with a glowing gas fire and ushered him onto a worn floral sofa. Several religious prints scattered the walls.

"There's a chill in the air," she said, rubbing her hands together. "Can I get you some tea?"

"No, thank you. I've left my dog in the car, so I mustn't be long."

"Well, what can I do for you, Detective?" Maureen smiled.

"Did you know that Father Brian was ill?"

"No… he always looked a picture of health."

"How long was it before you arrived at the church after the explosion, Maureen?"

"Just a matter of minutes, I think. But I had to use the side entrance as the front door was bolted from inside."

"Did you move the body at all?"

She hesitated. "I may have adjusted the Father's robes slightly to allow him some dignity... you understand. Then I quickly shouted for help outside the door and I think someone at Saxon Meadow called an ambulance."

"Of course; and I expect you had a little tidy up too, didn't you?"

She nodded sheepishly. "It was a terrible chaos."

"Tell me, Maureen – are you having difficulties with your sight today?"

"Yes, my cataracts... I'm feeling my age today," she said sadly.

Jonah thanked her, recommended she look after herself and headed back to the station.

"DI Jonah speaking. Oh, *hello* Jenny!"

"I've managed to get you an appointment with the Dean. Tomorrow you can see where the Episcopal polity meets in the cathedral and you can ask questions about the Archdiocese."

"That's wonderful, Jenny, thank you," he said, aware of Charlie's sour expression.

Jonah replaced the receiver, but it rang again immediately.

"Is this DI Jonah?" a voice asked. "It's Co-operative Funeral Care here. We have a problem with Father Brian's body."

"How do you mean a problem?" Jonah asked.

"Well, despite our embalming techniques, the corpse is decomposing so rapidly, we might not have a body at all to bury on Monday."

Jenny was a vision waiting for him at the cathedral entrance. Jonah shadowed her slim form up a spiral staircase, walking sideways to accommodate his long feet.

The heavy wooden door at the top creaked as Jonah opened it for her. He was immediately struck by the grand wooden seats around the square of the room, each carved with a different emblem.

"Matt Rogers," said a man stepping out from behind the door.

He was short and of slim build, with a shock of dark hair which nearly touched the top of his dense black-rimmed spectacles. Jonah reciprocated the handshake, finding it difficult to hide his disappointment that Jenny hadn't warned him of their meeting.

"The Dean couldn't make it after all," Jenny apologised. "He was called away on urgent business. However, Matthew probably knows more about this room than the Reverend Spalding does. You see he's held private piano tuition here for over two years now."

A black and white print in the corner of the room suddenly caught Jonah's eye; it was something from the Old Testament, depicting Moses turning away from the Ark of the Covenant as God passed by. At the bottom of the page was boldly written: "*And He said, Thou canst not see My face: for there shall be no man see Me, and live.*" *Exodus 33.20.*

Jonah's mobile rang… it was Charlie, so he excused himself from the room swiftly.

"You were correct," Charlie said. "Eight-year-old Freddie McCormack was hit by a car outside the cathedral three months ago and was DOA at hospital. For some reason he decided to run out suddenly from his private piano lesson. Father Brian has been receiving treatment for chronic depression ever since the loss of his son."

"Thanks, Charlie."

"Also, I found an old map of St. Mary's which shows a vault in almost the exact location of the crater."

"I thought there might be; but I wonder what on earth Father Brian could have been looking for down there?"

"One last thing, sir... apparently the verger is dying.

When Jonah returned to the upper room he found the couple withdrawing from an embrace.

"I'm sorry to interrupt," he said. "I've had an urgent call to go to the hospital, Jenny."

Don't worry, Matthew has a student arriving soon anyway. Before you go, I want you to be the first to know about this," Jenny said, dangling the fingers of her left hand in Jonah's face. The sparkling diamond drew everything from inside Jonah into a thick soup.

"What a novel location for a music lesson," Jonah said, feeling certain his stomach had dropped out. "Thanks for your help, Jenny. As usual you've been a star."

He glanced once more at the print on his way out.

A small man dressed in black stood by the hospital entrance. "I'm David, the Rural Dean... could I have a word?"

Jonah moved to one side.

"I'm afraid I've just had to administer the last rites to Maureen Baker," he said.

"Oh dear; I'm very sorry to hear that," Jonah said.

"Listen, there is much you should know," David said, handing him a small piece of paper with an address in Tibet. "Unfortunately, I can't explain now as we are being watched."

"What's this about?" Jonah asked, looking about him furtively.

"Longchenpa has waited a long time for this and he will ensure that only good will come from it," he whispered. "There are many who would seek what Father Brian found to start a war, rather than to glorify God."

"Confound it man, I don't understand what the hell

137

you're talking about!" Jonah snapped. "What exactly did Father Brian find?"

"Look, for some reason Maureen has chosen you to tell… if you can reach her in time. I will be in touch with you when it's safe to do so."

"The corneas of Mrs. Baker's eyes have been burnt," the nurse said, carefully scrutinising Jonah's ID.

"Is this to do with her cataracts?" Jonah asked.

"No, this is something new. Dealing with her cataracts now would be pointless. Light can't reach her retinas because some sort of very severe recent damage has occurred."

"So, what's the prognosis?"

"Basically, she's blind," the nurse said. "But much more worrying, we believe she's suffering from some aggressive type of wasting disease."

"Hello Maureen," said Jonah as he opened the door to a private room.

Maureen's face lit up.

"I've been thinking about you Daniel; I want to tell you something important. I found an old casket lying next to the poor Father. It was very plain and made from some sort of bronze metal; I'd never seen it before."

"Why didn't you mention this previously, Maureen?"

"I know I should have; but I knew I shouldn't have looked inside the box. Once I did, God told me that I must hide it safely away. In the wrong hands, it could surely be used as a dreadful weapon and cause terrible destruction; just look what it did to the Father… and now to me."

The black and white print in the cathedral suddenly came alive in Jonah's mind.

"*Thou canst not see My face: for there shall be no man see Me, and live,*" Jonah said. "Where did you hide it, Maureen?"

"I know you'll do the right thing," she said, reaching out her hand to Jonah. "Promise me you'll place the casket into safe hands. It's hidden behind a loose red brick in one of the graves."

Jonah took her withered hand and thought for a moment. "Do you mean the old mounded graves near the yew tree?"

She nodded as her breathing became laboured.

"You know I heard angels weeping over the Father's dead body," she whispered through quivering lips. "I glimpsed eternity that day, like a pure and endless light. Woe is me for I am ruined... my eyes have seen the King, the LORD Almighty!"

Maureen's hand suddenly became limp. A shiver zigzagged down Jonah's spine.

Jonah flew through the hospital doors clutching a crumpled cigarette packet. The wind had whipped up, causing festoons of cloud to lurch across the sky like angry phantoms. Swifts careered around recklessly, hurtling themselves like airborne fish and screeching electronic alarms. He called the morgue and Jeff confirmed that there had also been severe damage to Father Brian's eyes. As he drove home, rain spilled from a gunmetal sky; *now* there's a storm coming, Jonah thought.

"I've a job for you, Labrador," Jonah muttered as he ushered Leo into the car.

At St. Mary's, Leo positioned himself beside the first tree in the church yard. He eventually joined Jonah under the giant Yew and quickly became interested in one of the brick graves. There was a magical feel to the air which reminded Jonah of treasure hunts in his grandmother's garden when he was young.

"What is it boy?" Jonah said, falling to his knees. "I always said you'd have made an excellent sniffer dog."

139

His fingers trembled as he rewarded Leo with some liver cake and held the earth-sodden metallic object in front of him. The dog looked at Jonah, suddenly lifting his chin to howl in a weird and solitary way. Jonah fled, hiding the box under his jacket as they dashed back to the car, like two fugitives.

Jonah placed the casket on his kitchen table. He was about to feed Leo when something caught his eye; in the half-light he could see a strange glow coming from beneath the box. He drew closer, fascinated by the simplicity and the feel of the ancient metal, burnished by the past. He carefully examined the ancient box, finding some old engraving underneath.

"All those laborious years learning Latin have paid off, Labrador," he said; his heart kicking like a baby in his chest. *"No man… shall see the face of God… and live,"* he whispered.

Jonah had wrestled with the choice between life and death on many occasions before. How time slips away swiftly when it comes near to the end, he thought. He couldn't contemplate a life without Jenny; the perpetual winter since she'd left had been unbearable. He put Leo outside to eat his supper then pulled the cork on a good bottle of red wine. He lit his first cigarette in three months, feeling the smoke curve lazily past his tonsils and the head rush he'd longed for. Before he released the box as evidence, he needed to look inside for himself… regardless of the consequences.

The next day Jonah tied Leo to the drainpipe outside the café. Two women at the next table cast anxious glances at the mysterious figure wearing dark glasses. With decaying flesh clinging tautly over gaunt cheek bones, Jonah realised he looked contagious. He quickly slid on leather gloves to

140

cover liver-spotted hands. He'd every right to be in the little café he told himself as he smoothed down his last few remaining clumps of hair; he'd grown up in this town. Sipping his espresso, Jonah gazed sadly out at festive lights dangling limply in rows along the high street.

He remembered how different it was when Jenny sat across the table from him with her brown eyes sparkling and dancing. He'd hate her to see this monster he'd become... he couldn't bear that. In his mind's eye he pictured her holding the heavy brass bell and shivering in the damp greyness, surrounded by the deafening shrieks of her class. She wouldn't see him, nor recognise him if she did, as he blew her a final kiss. She would never know the sacrifice he'd made to protect her.

The bell tower chimed four and Jonah rose slowly so as not to alarm the women. He dropped some coins jangling into the saucer, guessing they'd be washed before going in the tips box. He untied Leo, leaning heavily on the white stick as he crossed the road to the cathedral. It had stood for centuries and he knew it would remain standing long after he and his Jenny turned to dust.

Jonah spied her over the wall. She was a vision in her yellow raincoat against the sepia surroundings... a beautiful sunflower. She might be lonely for the rest of her life; she might be 'an old maid' as she'd often feared; but at least she wouldn't be condemned to a life with a monster hiding behind her respectability as he preyed on the young boys he taught.

He tried to stop his hands from trembling as he took a call. "The package is airborne," said a voice. Intense relief flowed over him as he heard that the casket was safely on the plane to Tibet.

"Thank you, David," he said. "I'm on my way to the station now. Promise me you'll take good care of my Jenny;

she'll need your support if she's going to get through all this."

He glanced back one more time at Jenny, wishing he could spend his final hours in her arms. But there was still one more thing to do.

As he appeared at the station door, the room fell silent. Fully aware of the sudden changes in his appearance, Jonah limped over to Charlie. "A good sniffer dog," he said, calmly handing her Leo's lead.

He attempted to straighten himself as he entered the Chief Inspector's office.

"I've come to give my final report on the death of Father Brian, Sir," he said.

"I've just finished reading the report you emailed me last night," the CI said.

"But this is an important sub-text." Jonah took a deep breath, leaning heavily on his stick. "David, the Rural Dean, has been gathering evidence against Matthew Rogers for some time; he'd always suspected his sexual abuse of young choristers at St. Cuthbert's. Here are statements from four pupils, and there are many more. I've promised Ellen McCormack that Freddie's death will not be in vain; the boy was hit by a bus when he ran from Rogers at the cathedral and his father died seeking the truth."

"You look sick, Daniel… let me get you some help," urged the CI.

The papers Jonah held slipped like an injured bird through his fingers.

"How on earth did you make all these connections, Jonah?"

"It's a long story," he gasped. "But let's say… I've seen the light."

His tall frame crumpled to the floor like a marquee without any tent poles.

Everything has Changed

We scattered your ashes in your favourite meadow; the sky was painted with tears. There were only a few poppies in the hedgerows, so we sprinkled poppy seeds mixed in with you. Like the first smattering of snow it powdered the nettles and wild grasses under the weeping ash tree, making their heads bend in reverence. The breezes will come soon and pick up and dust you into the atmosphere, spreading you far and wide, dancing across the fields we walked in. It will float you into the streams you swam in, where you emerged with your glistening coat, shaking droplets of water multi-coloured with every spectrum of a rainbow.

Everything has changed

I will try not to look at dead things anymore… at static coloured moths and birds that no longer fly; try not to think of how beautiful they were when they were alive. I must focus my brain away from the pain of those last moments we spent together. Sometimes I feel so alone as I walk, like I'm missing an arm or a leg. But you were so brave, and I know I must be too.

Everything has changed

The nights are lighter now after suffering many long dark winter nights. You should be running and bobbing up happily through the wheat fields with your ears like errant wings. Always mischievous, always kind-hearted; my loyal best friend and trusted companion. Guardian angel on all our walks, your tail went poker straight upwards when you saw a suspicious person; a sudden warning bark… a cocky swanky walk towards them like your body was formed of rubber. Every day was an adventure we shared; finding pheasants to flush out, or partridges, or even ducks! Your face emerging through the long grasses behind me, running and jumping through the corn, a large toy pheasant held proudly in your soft mouth after a retrieve. I'd whistle you back from chasing deer or that shabby old wily fox that teased you, summoning you to go down flat to the ground when danger lurked. When I had a treat in my hand, you'd prance like a little pony beside me, eyes focused the whole time on mine. They said you were pedigree, named you Moreena Velvet Sunset, and you became a Kennel Club gold awarded dog; but you were just my old Tabitha dog really. Your brilliant hips allowed both hind legs to stretch out behind you like a frog on the carpet, forcing me step over you as I went from room to room. I love you for so many things but mainly the way you've always been beside me... a companion in whatever I did.

Everything has changed

I stoop as I walk under the apple tree, laden with summer promise. The fruit are only tiny now, but I remember your gleeful early morning face as you spotted a windfall through the glass patio door. I didn't know you wouldn't see the apples ripen this year or get those tufty darts stuck in your fur as the wheat turned to gold. I look for signs of you as I walk through the meadow but there are no new poppies there, just the change of the seasons.

Everything has changed.

It's been nearly five months and the summer has got the urge to go. I've walked alone on many bright summer nights, watching the crimson sunsets lengthen my single shadow across the meadow. I still picture you walking beside me or running ahead after a pheasant. I can still feel the shape of your head when I stroked you and that lovely thick fur you had beneath your neck. I must have vacuumed up every last dog hair of yours from our home now. As the golden hue of autumn approaches, I imagine you galloping through russet leaves as they play ring-oh-the-roses in circles on the ground. My life will be forever autumn, the winds will be much harsher, with only the early evening moon looking down like a ghost from the sky to keep me company; a crochet doily all alone like me.

Everything has changed

I wear smarter clothes these days, instead of the dishevelled multi-pocketed jeans splattered with mud and the coat with multiple pockets for treats and poo bags. My walking boots are stored away, pristinely cleaned and polished. My walks are along concrete streets and roads now, going to all the places that you hated; storing those country walks to my cherished memories. I miss them; and I enjoyed being my old scruffy self. Life was so different then.

They say that change is good, and it's true the pain no longer cuts so deep to make my heart bleed. Yet I know that wherever I walk, I'll always be walking with you. I will try not to go back to that dreadful night when you stopped the kitchen clock at 2.50 a.m. to say goodbye... until we meet again dear faithful friend; *everything has changed.*

About the Author

Jeanne Davies has always enjoyed writing fiction and her children grew up with ad-lib stories (sometimes scary!) at bedtime. In recent years more and more of her short stories have been published in anthologies, including some award-winning flash fiction and even poetry. One of her stories was recently included in an anthology published in the USA, with another being taken for their next publication.

Find More of Jeanne's Stories

Transforming Communities

edited by Debz Hobbs-Wyatt and Gill James

Transforming Communities was the theme of the 2020
Waterloo Festival Writing Competition. It is also the title of
the e-book that contains the winning entries. We chose these
because they tell a good story, have a strong voice, and are
imaginative in their interpretation of the theme. The writers
present us with characters that are believable and rounded.
The stories all contain a pleasing narrative balance.

Entrants were asked to produce a short story or a monologue
in 1,000 words or fewer. Less is certainly more here. Style
is diverse and each story is completely different from the
others.

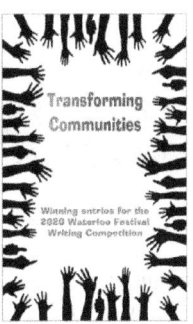

Order from Amazon:

eBook: ISBN 978-1-907335-84-6

Nativity

edited by Debz Hobbs-Wyatt and Gill James

Many of the stories in this collection take place at or near Christmas time. There are stories of new births, of rebirths, of new beginnings, and there are a couple that deal with the joys and sorrows of the annual Nativity Play.

There are some familiar authors in this volume and also some new writers. We treasure them all.

"A most unexpected collection of stories, focused on new beginnings and rebirth. It's definitely not your traditional nativity theme, but so much more. The stories are so varied, dramatic, melancholic, dark and comedic, there is a story to suit everyone." (*Amazon*)

Order from Amazon:

Paperback: ISBN 978-1-907335-76-1
eBook: ISBN 978-1-907335-77-8

Some of Our Other Single-Author Collections

Tales from Where the Wall is Cracked

by Paul Bradley

In this debut collection of short stories Paul Bradley takes a look at how extra-ordinary everyday life can be. Kitchen sink realism, magic realism and humour are deployed to present a variety of characters, many of whom live on the margins and cannot or will not fit in. In these pages you will meet a walrus man, a mynah bird called Hitler, Kendo Nagasaki, gypsy Romana, a lonely signaller and many others in an eclectic variety of edgy tales from where the wall is cracked. Wherever possible, light shines through.

"Thoroughly enjoyable from beginning to end with each story bringing the seemingly ordinary to very colourful life. Original, quirky, funny, thought provoking... and more. Definitely recommend!" (*Amazon*)

Order from Amazon:

Paperback: ISBN 978-1-907335-74-7
eBook: ISBN 978-1-907335-75-4

The Power of Love

by Phyllis J. Burton

The stories in *THE POWER OF LOVE* are quite simply about LOVE of all kinds. If you like romance, then these short stories are written just for you as well. There is plenty of that! The huge clock on Waterloo station acts as catalyst for that. But the collection also shows us other sorts of love: family ties, enduring love, old love, forbidden love, mended love, children's love for their parents, parents' love for their children, a love for old buildings, and love between animals and humans.

"If you're looking for short stories to read then look no further. These are great reads from Phyllis. The stories are tender, loving and well-written. I'd recommend these stories to everyone." (*Amazon*)

Order from Amazon:

Paperback: ISBN 978-1-907335-72-3
eBook: ISBN 978-1-907335-73-0

Other Ways of Being

by Gill James

Other Ways of Being is a an anthology of stories that point us to other times, other histories, other worlds including those of our near futures, other sexualities and other genders.

Order from Amazon:

Paperback: ISBN 978-1-907335-67-9
eBook: ISBN 978-1-907335-68-6